Jess Carter

and the Rodneys

Also by Geoffrey Lewis:

The Jess Carter Canal Books:

Jess Carter & The Oil Boat   978-0-9564536-1-7
Jess Carter & The Bolinder   978-0-9564536-2-4
Jess Carter & The Rodneys   978-1-909551-00-8

The Michael Baker Canal Series:

A Boy Off The Bank   978-0-9545624-6-5
A Girl At The Tiller   978-0-9545624-7-2
The New Number One   978-0-9545624-8-9
Cattle & Sheep & Boats   978-0-9564536-3-1

The David Russell Crime Stories:

Cycle   978-0-9545624-3-4
Flashback   978-0-9545624-0-3
Strangers   978-0-9545624-1-0
Winter's Tale   978-0-9545624-2-7
Gameboy   978-0-9564536-5-5

Other Canal Books:

Starlight   978-0-9545624-5-8
L-Plate Boating   978-0-9564536-0-0
    (with Tom McManus)

And:

Thunderchild   978-0-9551900-6-3
    A children's fantasy adventure after the style of Tolkien
Remember Me   978-1-909551-22-0
    A short story collection (as S G Miles)

ISBNs listed are for printed books; for more information and ebook details please go to www.sgmpublishing.co.uk

Jess Carter

and the Rodneys

By

Geoffrey Lewis

ISBN 978-1-909551-00-8

First published in 2013 by

SGM Publishing
47 Silicon Court, Shenley Lodge, Milton Keynes MK5 7DJ
www.sgmpublishing.co.uk
info@sgmpublishing.co.uk

ABOUT THE AUTHOR

Geoffrey Lewis was born in Oxford, in 1947, and educated at the City's High School and Hatfield University (then a polytechnic). He has since followed a varied career, including spells as a research chemist, security guard and professional photographer. After many years in the motor trade, and eight years as the owner and captain of a canal-based passenger boat, he is now retired and concentrating upon writing.

After a childhood spent close to the Oxford Canal, his love of the waterways led him to live aboard a narrowboat on the Grand Union Canal for sixteen years. Now back on dry land, he lives in Milton Keynes, not far from the canal, and recently took on the duties of Captain on the historic pair *Nutfield* and *Raymond* which are to be seen at many waterways events through year.

He has been writing seriously since the late 1990s, and has a number of novels in print. He is also a regular contributor to *Classic American* Magazine.

Photographer, bell-ringer, real ale drinker and American car enthusiast, he is currently engaged upon a number of new writing projects, including a children's fantasy adventure trilogy after the style of Tolkein, of which *Thunderchild* is the first volume; and of course more stories set in the working days of England's canals!

Chapter One

A bright, clear Tuesday morning – or as bright and clear as it was possible to be under the eternal haze that hung over England's industrial heartland of Birmingham and the Black Country. The city and its environs were waking to another day, its denizens beginning to throng the shaded streets as they hurried to their daily labours; their destinations, the factories and workshops, were beginning to wake from their brief night-time silence. Boats were beginning to move on the Midland canals – many of them the simple cabin-less 'joey' boats used for local work, horse-drawn, some of them in long trains behind a grumbling diesel-engined tug; here and there the brightly-painted cabinsides of a long-distance boat began to gleam through the burgeoning light of the early-summer day.

'Wha' time is it?' Jess Carter sat up in his bed, blinking sleepily. The dimly-seen figure sitting on the edge of the cross-bed stretched and yawned:

'Toime we was oop!' Jess heard Luke's chuckle as he groaned and lay back down, reluctant to stir for their new day's work, reluctant to let go of the pleasant dream he had been enjoying before his companion's rising had woken him.

The two boys were sharing the back-cabin of their boat – the *Swan* was brand-new, a wooden, seventy-foot-long narrowboat purpose built to carry liquid cargoes on England's canals. It was tied up in the basin at the Springfield Works in Oldbury, a suburb of Birmingham, waiting for the dock hands to unload its first cargo of tar, which the boys had brought back from Uxbridge Gas Works. They had collected the boat from the yard there where it had been built for their employers, Thomas Clayton (Oldbury) Ltd, and the tar had been loaded before their trip home – now it was to be discharged, and they would return to their regular work, carrying fuel oil from Stanlow on the Manchester Ship Canal to the Shell works at Langley Green, close to where they were at that very moment.

On that weekly trip, they would be accompanied by Luke's mother and sisters; the *Swan* was a motor boat, fitted with a big Bolinder diesel engine, powerful enough to tow another unpowered boat behind it. That butty boat, the *Tove,* was home to Annie Kain and her daughters – Alice was twelve, and Rosie nine – and all were waiting for them at Clayton's own yard, a scant hundred yards or so along the Birmingham Canal. Luke, oldest of the Kain children, was fifteen, and the nominal captain of the pair of boats – Clayton's were perhaps a little old-fashioned and would not allow a woman to be captain, so he had taken over after his father's death the previous winter, successfully convincing his bosses that he was actually sixteen and so eligible for the job!

Now, he shrugged into his shirt and pulled on his heavy moleskin work-trousers, and sat down again to push his feet into a pair of thick socks and his old but well-polished boots. Jess, half-dozing still, blinked again and pushed himself upright as Luke slid the hatch back, opened the cabin doors and stepped out into the early morning. Jess swung his feet to the floor and

8

reached for the kettle, standing ready-filled on the cabin stove; he groped for a box of matches, struck one and lit the newspaper and kindling in the fire-box, smiling to himself as wisps of smoke curled from the various cracks and joints of the miniature range which was their source of cooking, and of warmth in the cold weather.

He'd slept soundly, exhausted after a somewhat riotous evening in the company of the other Clayton's boaters at the yard and their eventful trip from Uxbridge. He was used, now, to curling up on the narrow side-bed of a boat's cabin, less than two feet wide and barely long enough for his thirteen-year-old frame to stretch out. Cramped, maybe, but far more comfortable than sleeping rough as he had been before the Kains had found him one misty morning under a railway bridge in Tipton – could it be barely three weeks ago? In that short time he had been accepted, informally adopted, into their life and world on the canal – accepted for who he was by people who had no concern for the colour of his skin. His black Jamaican mother had died some years ago; and the English father he loved dearly but regarded with a resigned tolerance was presently spending a few years 'at His Majesty's pleasure' after being caught acting as getaway driver for a gang of bank-robbers. The result of their ill-fated marriage was now a tall, slim and handsome boy with skin the warm colour of milk chocolate, sleek, glossy black hair and deep, dark eyes.

The kettle began to sing softly on the stove; Jess stretched again and reached for his shirt. Slipping it around his shoulders, he stood up and bent to look in the

9

cupboard below the drop-down table for the small saucepan they'd been using to brew tea – it had been a continuing source of self-deprecatory amusement to them both that they had never managed to acquire a proper tea-pot since picking the boat up over a week before. He ladled two scoops of tea into it and placed it on the stove next to the kettle, and then sat down again to pull on his trousers and socks.

Steam began to swirl from the spout of the kettle; he poured the hot water over the tea-leaves and left it to brew while he put on his boots. A few moments later, he pushed the cabin doors open again and stepped out, two steaming mugs in his hand:

'Luke – 'ere yeh go.'

'Taa.' Luke was standing on the dockside by the stern of the boat; he gestured across the dock to the factory buildings: 'The men're just gettin' in, moost be 'bout seven o'clock. We're 'ead o' the queue now, we'll be back ter the yard 'fore long.'

His prediction proved true – barely an hour later, they were backing the long boat out of the dock, riding high out of the water, relieved of its twenty-two tons of tar. Jess had watched in fascination as the dock men had pumped out the majority of their cargo and then used a hissing, writhing steam-hose to soften and liquefy the remainder, leaving the covered holds clean and ready for their next load. Now he stood on the gunwale at Luke's side, listening to the steady beat of the big single-cylinder engine as the *Swan* eased back along the dock, out into the junction where they had turned off from the main line of the canal.

At Luke's gesture, he hurried forward along the deck, picked up the long shaft and used it to push the boat's fore-end around. Under its influence, with Luke using the power of the engine to drive the stern in the opposite direction, they were soon facing east in the direction of Clayton's yard; Luke waved him to rejoin him at the stern, and handed him the tiller as he stepped onto the counter:

''Ere y'are, Jess – yew tek it in.'

'Yeh sure? You ortta be the one...' But Luke just gave him a curt nod:

'Go on! 'Oo's the captain 'ere, eh? Do as yeh're told!' But the huge grin on Luke's face belied the harshness of his words; he burst out laughing as Jess gave him an uncertain grin back.

Both of them were still laughing as Jess ran the boat alongside the wharf at Clayton's yard, skilfully reversing the engine to bring it to a gentle halt next to where their butty stood waiting for them. Luke's mother, watching their approach, lifted the fore-end line from the foredeck, held the boat in and tied it to an adjacent ring on the wharfside; Luke himself stepped off the stern and did the same there. With the boat securely moored, Jess climbed down into the engine-room and stopped the motor; in the sudden hush, the sound of men working on a docked boat under the roller-mounted sheds on the yard could be heard.

'Where's the girls?' Luke asked his mother.

'Alice is down the shops, gettin' soom stooff fer ar trip – Rosie's off playin' wi' the Beechey kiddies. She'll coom when she's called!'

'Ah. Mister Beechey's 'ere, is 'e?'

'Joost back from emptyin' at Langley. 'Is pair's at t'other end o' the yard.' She gestured along the wharfside.

'Tha's good! Oi wants ter 'ave a word wi'im, get soom tips about workin' a pair o' boats.' She laughed:

'Best get 'n catch 'im then! Yeh knows Abel, 'e won't be 'angin' about!' Luke grinned:

'Aye, roight! Coom on, Jess.'

***

'Mornin' Mrs Whelan – how're you today?'

Eight-thirty, and John Marsden's butcher's shop in Dock Street had been open since seven, as always. Ellesmere Port had risen to a bright spring morning - trade had been steady, and now Wendy Whelan stood at the counter:

'Morning John – we're all fine, thank you. Have you got a nice piece of pork for Matt's dinner tonight?'

''Course! How about this?' The butcher indicated a rolled belly of pork under the glass of the display: 'Be nice stuffed and roasted.'

'Yes, that'll do fine, John. About a couple of pounds, then it'll do cold for tomorrow too.'

'Right-oh!' Marsden turned away to chop the roll of pork belly in two at the wooden block behind him, still talking over his shoulder: 'Matt on duty today?'

'He's in the station, in charge for today.'

'They had any luck with the kid who's been pinchin' from the shops 'round here?'

'Not yet – no-one knows who he is, or got a good look at him. Matt's got his men on the lookout, though.' Marsden slapped the wrapped pork on the counter in front of her:

'There y'are. Anythin' else today?'

'That bacon looks nice, John – how much is it?'

'One 'n six a pound. It is good – had some for my own breakfast!'

'Go on, I'll have half a pound, then!'

'How's the kids doing?' Marsden picked up the slab of bacon and took it along to the slicer at the far end of the shop. He dropped it into place and switched the machine on as Wendy followed him along:

'They're well – Mark's in school of course, and Janey's at work.'

'How's she enjoying it – doing well?'

'Yes – she's...' Wendy turned at the sound of the bell that announced the opening of the shop door; Marsden too looked up:

'Hello – hey! Stop!' A tall skinny boy in grubby clothes had grabbed the wrapped roll of pork and snatched the door open again before it could shut fully. Wendy made a grab for him but only managed to brush the sleeve of his threadbare jacket before he was gone; Marsden left the slicer running and ran out after him:

'STOP! STOP THIEF!' He ran along the street towards Porter's Row, but the boy was too fast for him, impeded by his long butcher's apron. The boy

13

disappeared into Church Street, and Marsden gave up, walking furiously back to the shop where Wendy stood perplexed and angry:

'No good?'

''E was too quick for me.' The butcher was breathing heavily: 'Went into Church Street, towards the town. But I reckon he's from the dock, gone that way to fool us.'

'Why do you say that John?'

'You saw him! Grubby kid, scruffy clothes – and he looked kind of brown, tanned, like he lives outdoors, you know?'

'On the boats, you mean?'

'Yes, I reckon so. Poor town kids are all pale and pasty, if you know what I mean? And there's no farms that close here, are there?'

'I see – what are you going to do?' Marsden shrugged:

'Report it, I suppose. What else can I do? But your bit of pork's gone, I'm afraid!' He took the remaining half of the pork belly from the display and quickly wrapped it; he handed it to her with a rueful grin: 'There y'are Mrs Whelan! Can't have our local copper going hungry, can we?'

Chapter Two

Pointed in the right direction by a smiling Sue Beechey, Luke and Jess found the short, stocky boatman in the engine-room of his motor boat, an oily rag in hand, going around the massive bulk of the engine wiping down all of its highly-polished copper and brass fittings. He looked up as Luke knocked on the cabin-side:

'What? Oh, 'ello Luke, 'ow are yeh boy?'

'We're foine, Mister Beechey. 'Ave yeh got a minute?'

'Yeah – the Missus is doin' the washin' 'fore we lets go fer the Port agen.'

'Ah – she told oos where ter foind yeh!' Beechey grinned, wiped his hands on the rag and climbed out onto the dockside as Luke stood back out of his way. He sat on the edge of the boat's decked-over hold and waved the two boys to join him:

'So – yeh wants soom tips, Oi s'pose?' Luke laughed:

''Ow d'yeh guess?' Beechey clapped him on the back:

'Oi said as yeh'd end oop wi' a motor, didn't Oi? 'Ow did yeh get on wi'it on the way 'ere?'

'Great! Ain't it, Jess?' Jess nodded eagerly:

'Yeah! It's so fast arter an 'orse – 'n yeh feel more in control, some'ow. Leastways I do.'

''S'roight. Injun's loike an 'orse, 'n all – look after it, 'n it'll look after you; tek care of it 'n it won't let yeh down, roight?'

15

'Yeah! My Dad says the same.' Jess grinned his agreement.

'Broke down at Grove, on ar way back though' Luke added.

'Top seal. We 'eard 'bout it!' Beechey chuckled: ''Appens, wi' a Bolinder. Yeh watched what the man did ter fix it?' Jess nodded again; the boatman asked him: 'Could yeh do the same?'

'Mebbe – yeah, I reckon I could, if we 'ad the bits 'n the tools.'

'All yeh needs is a coupl'a spanners, the big'un fer the top bolts 'specially. 'N the stores'll give yeh a coupl'a spare seals if yeh arsks 'em. Then if it 'appens agen yeh can fix it yerselves. Don't tek long.'

'H'okay, we'll get soom.' Luke agreed; he asked: 'What 'bout the tricks o' workin' a pair?' Beechey laughed:

'Yeh can't expect me ter tell yeh all me secrets, now can yeh?' Luke looked crestfallen:

'S'pose not...' But the boatman, still grinning, took pity on him:

'Yeh'll foind ways that work fer you, as yeh goes along, boy. Yeh've seen oother pairs workin', 'aven't yeh?'

'Yeah, 'course.'

'Moine 'n all, eh! Yeh knows 'ow ter breast 'em oop?' Luke nodded: 'Yeh'll only breast 'em fer Northgate, 'n the riser at Bunbury – rest o' the way it's easier ter keep 'em single, wi' a twelve-foot snubber 'tween the locks 'round Beeston 'n down inter Chester. Watch out fer the Iron Lock – soides 'ave coom in agen,

16

'n it's real toight. Yeh moight get 'em in tergether – if they'll go in empt 'n down'ill, they'll go in loaded on the way oop.'

'H'okay, thanks – what about the narrer locks this soide o' Nantwich? 'N 'Ampton twenty-oone?'

'Yeh'll 'ave ter roon 'em single there!' They all laughed at the obviousness of the boatman's comment:

'I'd never 'ave guessed!' Beechey gave Jess a playful cuff on the ear:

'Get yerselves a 'undred-foot loine, roight? Coomin' oop, yeh teks the loine round the lock so's yeh can pull the butty in wi' the motor. Goin' down, s'easier ter bow-'aul it, wi' the boat empt. Quicker, 'n all. Teks longer, workin' the locks twoice, but the motor'll mek oop fer it on the long pounds; yeh can go a lot quicker there than an 'orse!'

'H'okay – thanks, Mister Beechey. Coom on Jess, let's go ter the stores.'

'Aye – see ol' Bernie there, 'e'll know what yeh needs. One oother thing?' Luke paused in the act of standing up:

'What's that?'

''Ave yeh been usin' a strap in the locks or reversin' the h'injun?'

'Reversin' it' Jess told him.

'Got the drop o' that, 'ave yeh?' Both boys nodded: 'Watch that, young feller – if it goes cold, it'll stop on yeh. Better ter use a strap ter stop the boat, 'specially where the locks're close.'

'Yeah – that 'appened a coupl'a times on the way 'ere' Jess told him. The older boatman nodded:

'Keep a strap 'andy on the starn-end, use it loike yeh did fer the 'orse. 'N use a flush from the paddles ter stop the boat goin' up'ill, roight? Joost loike yeh did wi' the 'orse-boat.'

'H'okay.'

But the look that Luke gave Jess as they headed across the yard to the stores suggested that he thought he knew better, that he perhaps regarded Beechey's last advice as a denigration of his ability to handle the boat and its Bolinder.

***

Police Sergeant Matt Whelan stood in John Marsden's shop, waited until the butcher had served his customer. Marsden turned to him:

'Hello Matt. Sorry to cause you more work!'

Whelan smiled:

'Not your fault John! This kid's getting to be a real nuisance.'

'Yeah. He's had stuff from me before, once, and from Ed Jones's greengrocers.'

'And from the bakers in Queen Street. But no-one's managed to catch him, or even get a really good look at him. He's had a younger kid with him sometimes, distracting the shop-keeper while he snatches what he wants, but I'm sure it's the same lad behind it. I've had everyone keeping an eye out, but we don't know who we're looking for.'

'Always food, isn't it? Petty stuff, really – but it's getting out of hand, Matt!'

'Yes, I know!' Whelan sighed: 'Wendy said you think he's from the dock, off a boat?'

'I could be wrong, Matt – but he's scruffy, dirty-looking, rough old clothes...'

'Could just be a poor kid from town?' Marsden shook his head:

'I thought he had a kind of fit, outdoor look about him, you know? Townee kids are all pale as a rule. This lad's dark, very tanned, black haired. And he can't half run!' Whelan nodded:

'You could be right, John. The reports I've had seem to come in regular little clumps, a few days apart. If he is off the boats, that would fit.'

'Yes, it would, wouldn't it?' Whelan sighed again:

'I'll get down there, try my luck! But you know what those people are like – I don't suppose they'll tell me even if they know who he is. Judging from the amount of stuff he's nicked, he's probably selling at least some of it on the cheap.' Marsden gave him a sympathetic grin:

'Good luck!'

***

To an observer on the bank, there appeared to be an air of carnival about the pair of empty boats as they swept past Horseley Fields Junction. A mechanic, peering out of the engine-room of a boat tied by the boatyard at Union Mills, gave them a cheerful wave and received a big grin and a happy ''Ow d'yeh do?' from the youngster at the motor's tiller; he turned back to his

19

task with a grin at the boy's obvious pride in the gleaming, just-docked appearance of his boats. Their paintwork shone bright in the late-afternoon sunshine, and the line of clean washing strung above the long deck of the butty from mast to cabin fluttered in the gentle breeze like celebratory flags.

Under Broad Street Bridge, past the cluster of old basins that served the centre of Wolverhampton, and Luke let the pair slide to a stop against the towpath above the top lock. They had set off a little over two hours earlier, fully equipped with all the extra lengths of rope needed for working a pair of boats – two hundred-foot towing lines, one for a spare; a short twelve-foot 'snubber' for working among the locks, various breasting lines and a pair of the cross-straps they were using at that moment to tow the empty butty. Pulled tight against the stern of the motor, the butty would follow inevitably without the need for someone to steer it, much like an articulated lorry on the road. And a new, small tea-pot sat on the range in the *Swan's* cabin...

While Jess leant his back against the motor's back-end rope looped around his waist, holding it in against the bank, Luke hurried to talk to his mother as she gathered in the now-dry clothes from the washing line. His sisters listened eagerly as Annie Kain asked her son:

'So 'ow're we gonna work these two down then?' Luke grinned:

'Jess 'n me've got it all sorted out, Ma. One of oos'll run the motor down, th'oother'll bow-'aul the butty 'n reset the locks in between. You 'n Rosie work the butty through, roight? 'N Alice can set ahead o' the

20

motor.' Annie gave him a long hard look, but then nodded, smiling:

'Yeah, roight boy. Tha's about what Oi'd thought too.' She looked around at her daughters and chuckled at their excited expressions: 'Wha's oop wi' you two?'

'We ain't never 'ad two boats ter work before, Mam!' Alice reminded her; she laughed:

'Yeh'll soon get fed oop wi' the extra work, mark moy words! 'Ere Luke, them's your'n 'n Jess's.' She handed a pile of folded clothes to him and waved him away to take them to the *Swan* while she disappeared into the cabin of the *Tove* with her own and the girls' things.

Alice ran forward to the first lock, beside its little cottage, but found that here at least she had nothing to do – the lock-keeper had seen them coming and was already pushing open the single top gate.

'Thank yeh, Mister Blake!' He grinned at her:

'Nao trouble, gal! Got yerselves a pair now then?' She nodded:

'Yeah! Ain't they loovely?'

'Very smart! Yew look after'em, now.'

'We will, Mister Blake!'

'Yeh've got a bad road, at least ter start. Beecheys went down a bit 'fore yeh.'

'H'okay!' Alice sounded unconcerned at this news; he chuckled, gave her a nod and retired to his garden, leaning on the gate to watch them.

Beside the *Swan,* Luke and Jess had held a hurried conference:

21

'You 'aul the butty, 'n Oi'll run the motor' Luke told his mate: 'We'll swap over 'alf way down, ter mek it fair, h'okay?'

'Okay' Jess agreed: 'Where abouts?'

'After 'leven. There's a big viadooct goes over, 'n the railway crosses roight below. Oi'll wait fer yeh ter catch oop.'

Chapter Three

Luke stepped onto the boat, stood in the hatches and pushed in the clutch. The *Swan* slid gently forward and into the waiting lock as Jess dropped the eye of one of the hundred-foot lines over the looby at the top of the *Tove's* mast. He dropped the still-coiled rope on the fore-deck ready to be used and walked to the lock, his windlass already stuck in the back of his belt.

Skilfully reversing the engine, Luke brought the *Swan* to a gentle stop, its stempost against the central mitre of the bottom gates. Pulling the clutch out, he stepped off onto the bank again and strode forward to lift the bottom paddles as Jess swung the top gate closed. The gate banged to, drawn the last foot or so by the flow of water; Alice had already hurried on down to the second lock, opening the paddles to fill it before the rush of water from the lock above could swamp the towpath.

In moments, the boat was dropping quickly into the chasm of the emptying lock. As soon as the water reached a level Luke, standing at the centre of the paired gates, kicked one open behind him and swung the other wide; he ran back and jumped down onto the boat, into the hatches again. With the engine running forwards again, he pushed the clutch in and ran the boat out, across the short pound and into the next lock as Alice swung the top gate wide in front of him.

As the *Swan* drew clear of the lock, Jess had already dropped the paddle on the side where he stood next to the bottom gates. He swung the one gate closed, ran across it and jumped the gap onto the other; pushing that one to, he dropped the second paddle and strode back to wind up a top paddle to refill the lock for the butty. Annie Kain had raised the other as he closed the gates; now, she stood ready to open the top gate once the lock was full, as Jess went to take the towline from the butty's fore-deck. As the gate swung open, he took the strain, the rope laid across his shoulders – behind him, the empty butty began to slide easily forwards, floating into the lock as he paced steadily along, Rosie steering it carefully into the narrow space barely inches wider than the boat. As she passed, she dropped the stern strap over the raised stump on the end of the open gate and caught it around the T-stud on the stern deck; the drag of the rope pulled the gate closed behind the boat and at the same time brought the *Tove* to a halt, nuzzling the mitre of the bottom gates.

In the lock below, the *Swan* was already descending as the water rushed out through the open paddles, pouring along the pound to fill the third where Alice stood by its own raised top paddles. Jess had come to a halt the length of the towrope below the top lock – now he dropped the rope where he stood and hurried down to be ready to close up and reset that one, while Mrs Kain waited to empty the butty's lock behind him.

And so they worked on, each knowing their job, each throwing themselves into it with the enthusiasm of people who love their work. Hardly a word was spoken – each knowing what each other would do, there was no need for communication; Alice, rushing ahead to fill each lock for the *Swan;* Luke, working the motor through; Jess, resetting each lock and bow-hauling the *Tove* between them; Annie Kain, working the butty through; and Rosie, steering the *Tove* along as Jess hauled and stepping off to help her mother at each lock.

After half a dozen locks, Jess's shoulders were beginning to ache, his legs starting to feel stiff. The butty, riding high and light in the water, took surprisingly little effort to haul along, but even so the unaccustomed, continuous effort was beginning to tell on his slim physique. It was a warm evening; he had already cast off his shirt and now wore only a thin singlet above the old work trousers that had been part of Luke's wardrobe. At lock nine, Luke noticed the growing weariness of his friend:

'Two more 'n Oi'll tek over, h'okay?' The amusement in his voice matched the grin on his face; Jess nodded with a rueful smile:

'Okay, thanks!'

Luke jumped down onto the boat and ran it forward. He had been using his skill at reversing the Bolinder to stop the *Swan* in each lock – but running at no more than tick-over speed, the big engine had gradually lost heat, its temperature dropping as time passed. Steering into the tenth lock, Luke worked the controls to reverse it again, but instead of the usual deep 'chuff' as it began to turn backwards, the Bolinder gave a desultory cough and stopped altogether. Carried by its momentum and deprived of its brakes, the boat swept on into the lock – he grabbed for the stern strap, laid on the cabin roof – too late! A loud BANG echoed back up the canal as the stempost hit the bottom gates.

Jess, in the act of raising the top paddles of the lock above, looked up at the sound. Remembering Abel Beechey's words, he suppressed a laugh at what he guessed must have happened; but he quickly ran down to make sure that Luke was all right, that no serious damage had been done. As he caught up with him, Luke looked around, his expression dark:

'Ruddy injun went out!' Stifling his grin, Jess asked:

'You okay?'

'Yeah, foine.' Luke sounded as angry as he looked; but then he caught the twinkle in Jess's eye, opened his mouth to make a sharp retort, but suddenly relaxed and chuckled instead: 'All roight! Oi should'a listened ter Abel. No 'arm doon – only ter moy proide! You go 'n look after the butty, Oi'll get this started oop agen. 'N don't you say a word ter the girls, roight?'

'Would I?' Jess let his grin show now; both of them burst out laughing as Luke waved him away and climbed down into the engine-room.

A couple of minutes later the Bolinder's familiar 'tonk-tonk-tonk-tonk' was again echoing around the locality. Jess and Luke quickly whipped up the bottom paddles of the lock; Jess stood ready to reset it for the butty which was already sitting in the bottom of the one behind waiting for them. He pushed open the bottom gates; Luke ran the *Swan* out and on to the next which Alice had left ready for him. Closing up, Jess hurried to refill the lock; once the top gate was open, he took up the *Tove's* towline and hauled it forward.

Two more locks, and as he'd promised Luke held the motor boat in the next so that Jess could take over:

'Oi've put the starn strap on the dolly, roight?' Jess looked and saw the short heavy rope coiled on the counter of the boat: 'Yeh drop it over the stump on the end of the gate as yeh goes by, roight? Whip it 'round the other dolly 'n it'll snatch the gate closed be'oind yeh. 'N if yeh've got it roight, it'll stop yeh 'fore yeh 'its the other gate!'

''Kay. Will yeh come ter the next'n wi' me 'n show me?' Luke gave him a stern look, but then he relented:

'Yeah, h'okay. Yeh're still larnin' ain't yeh?' he chuckled.

They quickly dropped the boat in the lock and opened the gates. Both jumped down onto the cabintop; Jess took the tiller and pushed in the clutch, while Luke stood on the gunwale at his side. As they approached the next lock, he began his instruction:

'Roight – get ready mate.' The fore-end nosed into the chamber:

'Tek the clutch out – pick oop the strap – now, whip it over that bit stickin' oop at the end o' the gate.' Jess did as he was told, looping the heavy line over the protruding stump at the gate's outer end: 'Now, catch it 'round the dolly – that's it – good'n, mate!'

Almost to Jess's surprise, it worked! The rope, looping from dolly to dolly on the boat's stern and caught around the stump pulled the gate closed behind him, slowing the boat's momentum and bringing it to a neat stop just before it touched the far gate. He looked up into Luke's grin:

27

'That's easy, ain't it?' Luke laughed:

'Yeah – but yeh've got ter get it joost roight! Too long 'n yeh'll 'it the bottom gate – too short 'n this gate'll jam yeh on the way in. Reckon yeh can manage it?'

'I can try!'

'H'okay Jess. Yew get on; Oi'll go back fer Mam 'n the butty.'

They completed the remaining locks of the Wolverhampton flight in less than an hour, with Jess' and Luke's roles reversed. Luke being older and more used to such work, Jess found that the butty was close on his heels all the way – but he refused to be rushed, rather taking his time in order to do the job with a degree of care. Even so, he only got the 'strapping-in' part of his task right in about half of the locks – several times, he left the rope a fraction too long, and gave the boat a nasty jolt as its stem-post hit the bottom gate; and then, trying too hard not to do that, he caught one too short and ended up with the rudder caught against the top gate as it swung in too closely behind him. And each time he got it wrong, he could see Luke's grin getting wider as he bow-hauled the butty into the lock behind him.

But it was still easier, in a way, than trying to reverse the engine each time. In the close confines of the locks, the juggling of levers that that needed took time, when split seconds made the difference between stopping in the right place and being too quick or too slow, stopping half-way into the lock or hitting the far gate. And if the Bolinder was likely to keep stopping on him because it was too cold – well, he'd stick to using the rope!

At last he ran the boat out of the final lock, heaving a sigh of relief. There was the little stop-lock at the next junction, half a mile on, but he knew from his last trip that there was a long way then with no locks at all. He let the *Swan* drift to a stop under the brick bridge which crossed just below, where Alice was waiting for him. Catching the back-end rope around a ring set there for the purpose, he gave her a grin:

'Come on, let's 'ave it ready fer'em!' They closed the bottom gates and hurried to the far end of the lock; Luke, already there, had one paddle raised as Jess ran across and wound up the other. He crossed back over to open the gate as Luke picked up the towline and began to haul the butty towards him, and in a matter of moments it was descending in the lock; the bottom gates open, Jess backed the motor in and picked up the cross-straps for the tow as far as their next turn and the stop-lock.

During their trip back from Uxbridge, the boys had been given an old but serviceable bicycle by the lock-keeper at Broadwater Lock in Harefield, and it had proved invaluable, enabling one of them to go on ahead and set each lock before the boat got there. Now, Luke pressed it into service again, lifting it from the deck of the *Swan* and swinging his leg over its crossbar:

'Oi'll see yeh at Autherley Stop!' And he was off, windlass tucked in his belt, over the bridge and into the distance.

Dusk was gathering; the two boats, now running together again like an articulated lorry, swung out into the Staffordshire and Worcestershire Canal, and turned northwards. Alice stood on the gunwale next to Jess – Annie Kain had stepped onto the butty as Rosie steered it out and around the turn, using its big wooden tiller to swing the stern clear of the bridge.

Chapter Four

Alice climbed up and sat on the edge of the cabin, giving Jess a big smile:

'It's good ter 'ave yeh back with oos, Jess.'

'It's good ter be back!' He echoed her smile: 'We got down them all right, din't we?'

'Yeah – but what were that loud bang, 'bout 'alf way down?' Jess chuckled:

'Don' tell Luke I told yeh! 'E'd been reversin' the engine ter stop the boat, but it 'ad got cold 'n wen' out on 'im! 'E 'it the bottom gates real 'ard. Din't do no damage, though.'

'Is that why yeh were strappin' it in after you took over?'

'Yeah. S'what Mister Beechey tol' us ter do, 'n 'e's right – it's easier 'n quicker ter do that.'

'S'what we've alwes done any'ow, when we 'ad Prince! Yeh managed it h'alroight?'

'Yeah, more or less! Got it wrong once or twice.' She smiled at him:

'Yeh're gettin' ter be a real boatee, Jess.' He felt a swell of pride at her words:

'Yeh reckon?'

'Oi do! Oi'm so pleased we got yeh with oos now, Jess.' She leaned over and gave him a quick kiss on the cheek. He grinned at her:

'Eh, don' do that, yeh'll put me orf!' She looked crestfallen, and he burst out laughing: 'Not while I'm steerin', anyway. Any other time's fine!' She brightened up again, and he reached out to put his hand

31

on her shoulder momentarily; now she flashed him a cheerful smile.

They rode on in a friendly silence to the left-hand turn that would take them onto the Shropshire Union Canal. Jess took the boat out wide to negotiate the corner, powering the *Swan* straight into the waiting stop-lock where Luke stood by the gate, ready to push it shut. Jess loosed off the *Tove*, kicking it back a few feet to clear the gate as Luke closed it. In moments, the motor boat was through; the butty followed, and they were on their way again with only a few minutes delay. Jess relinquished the tiller to Luke again, and sat with Alice on the cabintop as the dusk fell around them.

***

'That was good, Wendy!'
Matt Whelan sat back, patting his stomach appreciatively. His wife nudged her son:
'Take the plates out, Mark?' The teenager collected the crockery together and headed for the kitchen, balancing the pile carefully in his arms. His mother looked across the table:
'No luck with the kid who stole the meat?' Matt shook his head:
'No. I talked to some of the people at the dock, some of the boatmen, but no-one's saying anything.'
'You think John's right about him being off a boat?'
'It makes sense, Wen. His exploits come in fits and starts, as if he's not always here, and John reckons he's

32

got a really tanned outdoor look about him, so it would add up. But you know what those folk are like! They don't like us much, won't give a copper the time of day. Look how they closed ranks about that black kid, a few weeks ago? I still don't know if he was ever here!'

'What happened about him?'

'Oh, we had a message a few days later, saying the trouble had been sorted out. I don't know if they caught him, or if it was all a fuss over nothing.'

'John says the boaters are really nice people – he sees a lot of them in his shop.'

'Oh, they are! They're no trouble, as a rule, but they just keep to themselves, don't want anything to do with other folk. And you should see how they keep those boats – always clean and shining. I've been in the cabins of one or two over the years, and they're spotless inside too. Oh, you see the occasional scruffy one, but they're the exception rather than the rule.'

'A bit like Gypsies, then, are they?'

'In a way, I suppose. The same pride in their way of life, and the same tendency to shrug off the rest of the world and stay in their own, among their own people'

During the course of his enquiries around the extensive dock area, Whelan hadn't spotted the tall skinny kid in the hold of a tired-looking butty, helping to level the load of china clay. But the boy had seen him, and noted the sergeant's stripes on his uniform...

***

The *Swan* and the *Tove* spent that night tied side by side to rings set in the towpath close under a high bridge on the Shropshire Union Canal. Above them nestled the town of Brewood; adjacent lay two more pairs of boats, one Fellows, Morton & Clayton and one Midland & Coast, each in their distinctive liveries, both deep-loaded and clothed over in contrast to the empty Thomas Clayton pair with their flat, planked decks.

They had no need of the town, having bought provisions before leaving Oldbury; but boaters always preferred to tie in company, close to civilisation whether that was a town or village wharf or just a canal-side pub. Dinner had been eaten long ago, on the long pound before Wolverhampton locks; a supper of bread and cheese, a last mug of tea apiece, and they settled down for the night.

***

In the lower basin at Ellesmere Port, another pair of boats lay silent. They should have been well on their way, maybe beyond Chester, but the poorly-maintained Russell Newbery engine had finally refused to co-operate when the crew had been ready to leave, and now they awaited the attention of the fitter from the dock. He, it must be said, was in no hurry to attend these particular boats, unhappy at working on such dirty and poorly-looked-after vessels, and not convinced that he would get paid for his labours.

In the butty's cabin, Enid Hampson sat counting her meagre supply of cash – the extra they'd made from

34

selling half of that nice joint of pork had gone in Bert's pocket to the Canal Tavern, and she knew there would be none left for buying provisions, or a new pair of shoes for little Jimmie, by the time he returned. But they'd eaten well – the other half of the pork had cooked up nicely, stewed with plenty of vegetables in the big pot on the range. And there was enough left over for tomorrow, too. She gave a sigh, and put her purse out of sight at the back of the table-cupboard. Letting down the cross-bed, she got herself ready for sleep, casting a last glance down at seven-year-old Maggie, curled up sound asleep on the side-bed.

'Stop yakkin' 'n go ter sleep!' In the motor's cabin, her three sons were settled for the night – or would be, if Jimmie would stop talking. Joe, his older brother, turned his back to the ten-year-old, sleeping next to him in their cross-bed. On the side-bed, Bert junior was already asleep, snuffling quietly.

Chapter Five

During the night, cloud had gathered, and the boating world awoke to a steady drizzle. At Brewood, Annie Kain and her children – she had come to regard Jess as her honorary son now – enjoyed a hot mug of tea while the boys checked over the Bolinder engine and got it started for their day's journey. They had agreed a turn-and-turn-about system again for themselves, after the complications of 'Hampton flight the day before, and Jess stood proudly at the tiller, his old work-coat tight around his shoulders, his flat cap drawn down over his eyes, as they travelled the three miles to the village of Wheaton Aston and its single lock.

The pair was quickly through, and with the water-cans topped up from the nearby tap, they settled down for the long pound to Tyrley locks, seventeen and a half miles away. Jess alone stood out in the rain, the cabin doors pulled closed behind him, the slide hatch against his tummy keeping the worst of the weather out of the cabin. Luke had lit their stove before they set off, and now its gentle warmth close to his legs seemed to dispel the drab chill of the day so that he felt contented with his lot, the tiller quivering in his hand, the deep, regular throb of the Bolinder in his ears. Behind him on its cross-straps, the butty followed obediently; every now and then, the hatch would slide back, and Alice's blond hair would appear momentarily, making sure that all was in order before disappearing below again into the warmth of the cabin where her mother was preparing the stew-pot for their dinner.

***

Constance and *Prudence!* Mike Parker thought he had never seen boats so inappropriately named. Mike enjoyed the reputation of a first-rate man, even if he might shrug such an accolade off himself – working from his own small workshop behind one of the big warehouses of Ellesmere Port's extensive dock area, he could tackle any kind of repair jobs on the boats that used the dock, whether the big barges off of the river or the long-distance narrowboats that plied the canals. He knew his way around diesel engines, gearboxes, propeller shafts and couplings – and he was a past-master of improvisation, able to get even the most recalcitrant machinery running again.

He stood surveying the unkempt pair of boats before him: *What is it with Bert Hampson? How can he let a pair of nice boats get into this state?* The paintwork was all faded and peeling, the names of the boats and the legend "Herbert Hampson, Canal Carrier" barely readable; a tarpaulin drawn over the motor cabin told its own tale of a leaking roof. Everything about the pair spoke of neglect and dereliction – the cloths untidily roped down over the holds were patched and threadbare, hardly able to keep the cargo within dry. He drew a deep breath and knocked on the butty's cabinside...

***

37

The narrow locks of Tyrley, known to the boaters as 'Drayton Five', were quickly passed, the crew of the *Swan* and the *Tove* working together as they had the day before at Wolverhampton. With hardly a word spoken, they were heading off towards the town of Market Drayton with little more than a half-hour delay. The drizzle had finally stopped; dark clouds still streamed overhead, but now Alice and Luke sat on the cabintop of the motor, talking to Jess, their coats around their shoulders. Annie and Rose sat together in the stern well of the butty, the little girl watching and learning as her mother crocheted a strip of lace for the *Swan's* cabin, which still lacked much of the decoration that she regarded as essential for a civilised life.

In the slowly brightening day, they swept past the town, past the spot that Jess recognised where they had stopped overnight on the last trip, his first on the boats, where Luke had put off the policeman who had come to question him about their runaway companion. An hour after Tyrley, they were working just as quickly and efficiently down another five locks near the village of Adderley. Then another half an hour, and they were into the long flight of fifteen that dropped past the village of Audlem. Part of the way down, they passed the wharf, and Jess nudged his friend:

'Remember stoppin' 'ere las' time, on the way back?' Luke gave him a rueful grimace:

'Not 'alf! Oi can still feel the 'eadache afterwards!' Alice gave her brother a disapproving look as she went ahead to the next lock, and he laughed. Taken to the local pub by another Claytons captain, he'd come back rather the worse for wear, and suffered for it the following day:

'Won't be doin' that agen in a 'urry!'

***

'Well what can yeh do wi' it?' Bert Hampson (senior) sounded impatient.

'It needs a thorough overhaul, Bert. Strippin' down and refurbishin', new valves an' guides, mebbe new rockers. A rebore too, I expect.' Mike Parker stood within the engine-room of the *Constance,* looking up at the displeased boatman on the dock by its side.

'Rubbish! It's bin runnin' jus' fine fer ages!'

'That's the trouble, Bert' Parker held onto his own patience: 'It's been goin' for years without any proper maintenance, an' now it's had enough.'

'Oh come on, Mike! We ain't got the time fer all that, nor yet the money, you knows that! I've got a load o' clay on fer Middlewich, an' we'll lose the job if it ain't there on time!'

'I know...' Parker sighed: 'All right, Bert. I'll whip the front head off, that's where the big trouble is. Mebbe it's just a bit o' carbon stuck under a valve – if so I'll get it runnin' for yeh. But remember what I said – yeh need a complete rebuild – or a new engine. An' pretty soon, too.'

'Do what yeh can, then. We needs ter be away terday, though.'

39

'It'll take as long as it takes, Bert. But after lunch, mebbe?'

'All right!' Hampson stamped away angrily to his butty with the aim of telling Enid to get the kettle on and brew some fresh tea. His mood wasn't helped when he found she had anticipated him, and handed him a mug as he stepped into the well; he sat grumpily on the gunwale, sipping at the hot, sweet liquid, his head throbbing gently as a result of the previous evening's indulgence.

Down in the engine-hole, Parker set to work – he had already partly stripped the front one of the engine's two cylinders, knowing that that was where the basic trouble lay, and it wasn't long before he had the cylinder-head in his hands. As he'd suspected, it was coked up with heavy, black deposits of carbon, built up over years of running with no attention, and one of the valves was jammed partly open where a piece had broken away and lodged underneath it. It pained him to have to do a 'quick-fix' job when he knew the engine needed so much more – but he'd be lucky to get paid even for that, if he knew Hampson. He set about roughly cleaning the head and freeing the valve, aware of Hampson's oldest son crouching in the side-hatch watching him.

'You all right, Joe?' he asked.

'Yeah, not bad. Did yeh see that copper 'ere yestiday, Mike?'

'The sergeant? Yeah.'

'What did 'e want?'

'He was askin' about a lot o' stuff that's been nicked from local shops. They reckon it might be a kid off the boats who's been stealin' it.'

'Oh – right.' Joe pretended indifference: 'D'yeh wan' a cuppa? Ma's just brewed.'

'Please – that would be good!'

The boy strolled away casually, but his mind was revolving around what Parker had said...

***

The cloud was beginning to break as the tank-boat pair worked through the two locks of Hack Green, three miles north of Audlem. Another three miles, and they were passing the town of Nantwich, over the Chester Road aqueduct and past the junction which led to the town basin. Once again, the change in the character of the canal struck Jess – no longer the long straight channels of the many miles from Autherley Junction, now the cut was wider, sweeping around a succession of bends, some long and easy, others tighter where he could only see a short distance in front of the boat.

Evening was closing in as they passed the left-hand junction which led onto the Welsh canals, its flight of locks lifting away to the west. Slowing to allow another pair to take the turn, Jess let the pair drift along until the road ahead was clear before winding up the Bolinder to its full speed again. But as he did so, a frown crossed his face: *That don't sound quite right...* But the big engine kept up its steady beat, and he shrugged his shoulders.

A mile and a half further on, in full dark now, they reached the eastward junction of the Middlewich Branch at the village of Barbridge, and just past the wharf with its straddle warehouse he put the clutch out and slipped the towing straps, allowing the butty to slide up alongside. Snatching the boats together, they tied for the night on the towpath.

Supper was eaten in a mood of quiet self-congratulation. Luke and Jess, and it seemed Annie Kain too, felt that the five of them were working well together as a team in the unfamiliar task of running a pair of boats. Two days had seen them cover as much ground as they might have done before with the *Murray* and Prince – no mean achievement as they'd had to work every lock twice this time. The faster speed of the motor boat had made up the difference, but they were still feeling very pleased with themselves!

They were still sitting gathered around the stern well of the *Tove* when the sound of an engine disturbed the quiet. Jess looked around:

'Who's goin' at this time o' night?' Luke chuckled:

'There's some as'll go all noight if yeh let 'em!'

They watched the boats, deep-loaded, their holds clothed over, run past them, the engine now throttled back to a tickover; The steerer, a tall skinny teenager, raised a hand in greeting but didn't speak, and Jess waved back. Just beyond them, he put the motor into reverse and turned to gather in the towline as the butty drifted up to it. Even in the dark, the dirty, unkempt state of the pair was evident; Jess had become used to the normal boater's intense pride in their charges:

42

'They look a bit rough, don't they?' Luke had spotted the tired name on the cabinside:

'Yeah. Them's 'bout the roughest pair in this neck o' the woods.' Annie confirmed his opinion:

'Bert 'Ampson owns them boats 'imself, but 'e don' take any care of 'em. Does loads fer anyone 'oo'll give 'im one.'

'The kid steerin' looked about our age, Luke?'

'Yeah – that'll be Joe, the oldest.'

'You keep away from them Rodneys, Jess' Annie admonished: 'They ain't noice folks at all. Dirty as them boats are, 'n they'll 'ave anythin' away as ain't bolted down.'

'Oh – right. Rodneys?' The expression had puzzled him; Luke chuckled:

'Tha's what boatees call anyone loike them – dirty and dishonest, loike Ma says.'

'But why Rodneys?' Luke shrugged:

'Oi dunno; d'you, Ma?' She echoed his gesture:

'It's just what we calls 'em, Oi dunno where it coom from.' Jess had to be satisfied with that; he nodded and went back to his mug of tea.

43

Chapter Six

Thursday morning they were up and ready for the off as the Sun struck over the buildings of Barbridge Junction. An occasional lorry roared past them on the road that ran a few yards away from the canal, but otherwise all was quiet as Luke heated the blow-lamp to start the engine – there was no sign of life from the other pair of boats, tied between them and the turn onto the Middlewich Branch behind them. In daylight, they looked even worse to Jess – the paintwork drab, peeling and faded, the hulls knocked about, the cloths over the load dirty and torn: *Rodneys! Funny name, but it fits somehow...*

The Bolinder started at Luke's second attempt. Usually, it went first time, and Jess again had that vague feeling that it hadn't sounded quite normal as it finally gave its deep 'Booff' before settling to a steady beat, slowing to tickover as Luke wound the throttle back. With no locks for a while, Jess stepped onto the gunwale beside him as the motor slipped away:

'The engine don' sound right, Luke.' Luke, busy picking up the cross-straps from the butty's fore-deck to re-attach the tow, looked around at him:

''Ow d'yeh mean, Jess?'

'You remember when it gave out on us, on the way from Uxbridge? It sounded a bit like that when yeh got it started. 'N it didn't want ter go, did it?'

'Yeh reckon we moight 'ave trooble wi' it?' The tow attached, Luke settled to the tiller for his day's steering.

'Dunno – mebbe.'

'What d'yeh reckon we ortta do?' Jess shrugged:

'Keep goin' It's goin' now, let's get on – will we get ter Ellesmere Port terday?'

'Should do.'

'Ther's bound ter be someone there as can tek a look at it, ain't there?'

'Yeah. Moike Parker's one o' the best h'engine men 'round, least tha's what Abel Beechey says, we can arsk 'im.'

'Okay, let's go on then.'

Three miles on, they faced their first opportunity to breast the boats together to work them through the impressive two-lock staircase of Bunbury. Luke knew what was needed, had seen other boaters working pairs on many occasions – but he'd never had to do it himself. Approaching the first lock, he slowed the *Swan,* and unhitched one of the short straps towing the *Tove* so that it swung away to one side of his stern; and then as the boats entered the lock, he kicked off the other and reversed the engine. The *Swan* drew to a halt, nicely placed in the lock; the *Tove,* carried by its own momentum, slid up alongside, and he grabbed a short, stout rope attached to a big shackle on the butty's stern and dropped it over the stern dolly of the motor – it snapped tight, stopping the boats together as Jess and Alice heaved the gates closed behind him. He looked around with a grin:

'That went pretty well!' Jess grinned back as he hurried past to open the paddles and begin their descent;

Luke quickly tied his stern rope across to the butty's T-stud, holding the boats tightly together, and Jess jumped down onto the front deck to do the same there.

When the water levels equalised, they opened the centre gates and Luke ran the boats through into the second chamber, where again they dropped through quickly and easily. As the bottom gates opened he released the lines holding them together, and so singled out again, they travelled on. At Tilstone Lock, they worked through without breasting up, simply allowing the butty to run in alongside the motor and then picking up the tow as they left. Then the two adjacent locks of Beeston, the 'Stone Lock' first, and then the notorious 'Iron Lock' with its cast-iron chamber. Here, Luke ran the motor boat in alone, and then Jess took a rope from the butty to pull that in very slowly, mindful of Beechey's warning that the locksides had moved in, narrowing the top of the chamber; but it ran in easily, albeit with barely an inch to spare.

Minutes later they were on the way again, towards Wharton Lock, the last for about eight miles. Cycling ahead, Jess found his gaze drawn to the imposing bulk of Beeston Castle, towering on its crag less than a mile away to the south of the canal. He quickly had the lock set for the boats, and sat on a balance beam to wait for them, gazing across at the impressive bulk of the castle.

But his attention was drawn back to the canal as Luke ran the boats in, loosing the butty off and grabbing the breasting-strap from its stern, dropping it over the motor's stern dolly to stop its forward momentum as it floated past him. He had been reversing the engine to stop the boats in theses wide locks where strapping in was not an easy option; now he went through the procedure again, but the Bolinder was having none of it. It gave a loud, despondent cough and stopped altogether; the two boats, held together by the strap at their stern, drifted on to hit the bottom gates with double wallop – fortunately, he had already slowed them to a point where no damage was done, but he swore under his breath and looked at Jess with a rueful smile:

'It stopped' he said, rather superfluously; Jess grinned:

'Yeah, I noticed.'

'What 'appened?' Annie called from the butty's tiller.

'H'engine went out!' Luke called back: 'Oi'll get it goin' agen!' He dived down into the engine-room, where Jess joined him.

It was a repeat of their fruitless efforts the week before, at Grove Lock. Half an hour later, begrimed and annoyed, they emerged into the daylight, the Bolinder stubbornly silent.

'Well?' Annie asked her son; Luke shrugged:

'It won' go.'

'I can see that! What's wrong?'

'I reckon it's the top seal agen, like before' Jess told her: 'The man in the stores at Ol'bury said these engines'll do that when they're new. They gets over it when they're really settled down.'

'Yeah – s'what the man 'oo fixed it las' toime said an'all' Luke confirmed.

47

'Well, can yeh fix it, either of yeh?' Luke looked dubiously at Jess:

'Oi dunno...'

''Course we can! We got the bits 'n the tools from the stores, so's we could do it if we 'ad ter. 'N I watched the man las' time, so I knows what ter do.'

'Better get on wi' it, then' Annie told him.

'Er – yeah, right...'

''Ow mooch longer's it gonna take?' Jess rounded on his friend after he'd asked the same question for the umpteenth time:

'Don' rush me! If I gets it wrong, we'll really be in the shit, right? I'll 'ave it done soon – 'n done right, if yeh leaves me ter get on wi' it.'

They'd dropped the boats through the lock and hauled them out to leave the road clear for other traffic, and then Jess had set to work, laying out his tools and the spare gasket ready. Then, carefully, step by step, he'd followed the procedure he'd seen the mechanic from Uxbridge use to remove the various fittings before unbolting and removing the cylinder head. Despite his show of confidence in front of Luke and Mrs Kain, he felt very nervous at taking on what was a serious job like this one, in the middle of nowhere with no help at hand – he'd worked on engines before, but his father had always been on hand to advise him, and get him out of trouble if he needed it. He'd stood there for a moment, looking at the big single-cylinder engine, not far from being as tall as he was, studying what he needed to do, before plucking up his courage.

But then, taking his time, he soon had the head ready to come off; it took the two of them, wiggling it upwards between them, to lift it over the protruding studs, and then to drop it back into place with the new seal seated underneath it. Still working slowly and carefully, Jess replaced the big nuts which held it down, tightening them as hard as he could with the long spanner the storeman had recommended for the job. Refit the various control linkages, remount the blow-lamp, and they were ready to try it.

He stood clear, stretching his tired back, to let Luke light the lamp and begin the process. Soon he had the plug glowing red; he reached up to set the throttle, spun the flywheel to the compression point, and gave Jess a hopeful look as he threw his weight on the sprung pin. The engine turned over with a loud 'Duff!', but stopped before firing again, the flywheel rocking to a standstill.

'Try it agen Luke – it sounded all right ter me. Give it a bit longer wi' the lamp.' Jess advised.

Five minutes, and Luke tried again – this time, the Bolinder gave its habitual 'Bouff!', spun on, fired again, and settled to its normal steady 'tonk-tonk-tonk-tonk-tonk'. Luke heaved a sigh of relief and turned the throttle back, the engine slowing to its uneven 'tonk—tonk-tonk---tonk—tonk' tickover as if nothing had happened. He turned to Jess:

'Yeh did it, mate!' Jess was grinning too:

'Yeah! Knew I could, mind...'

'Ye-ah!' Luke's sceptical tone had them both laughing as they climbed out onto the bank.

'Well done, Jess – yeh do know summat 'bout these h'injuns then!' Annie congratulated him; Alice was there too, and flung her arms around him:

'Oi knew yeh'd do it, Jess!' He refrained from patting her back with his oil-grimed hands, receiving an approving chuckle from Annie; then Rosie too had to give him a hug and a big, happy smile.

Despite their congratulations, Jess was uncomfortably aware that they'd lost a large part of the day. He turned to Mrs Kain again:

'I'm sorry it took so long ter fix. I didn' want ter rush it 'n get anythin' wrong.'

'Don' worry Jess! Better ter 'ave it roight than be stoock 'ere 'n waitin' fer someone ter come 'n do it. We'd 'ave lost a lot more toime that way.'

'We'll never get ter the Port terday now though, Ma.' Alice pointed out.

'We can if we goes fer it!' Luke interjected, but his mother shook her head:

'No Luke – we'd be goin' 'til near midnoight, 'n Oi won't 'ave you workin' Northgate riser in the dark. Anywhere else, but not them locks. We'll get ter the top o' them, 'n stop there.' She turned to Jess: 'We've got a whoile now Jess – go in 'n boil a kettle, 'ave yerself a good wash 'n rest fer a bit. 'N thank yeh, boy – Oi'm pleased we got yeh with oos!'

'I'm 'appy ter be 'ere too, Ma!' He ducked down into the cabin with a full kettle as Luke went to untie the boats. Annie loosed off the sterns, and Luke steered the motor out, picked up the tow and set off towards Chester and their next locks.

Chapter Seven

The night spent at the top of Northgate locks again reminded Jess of his previous trip to 'The Port'. They had moored for the night there then, too. This time they had arrived quite late, tied up and fallen straight into bed – supper, bread and cheese and tea, had been eaten as they travelled through Chester, under the looming city walls.

In the morning, a quick start saw them down the dramatic descent and under the bridges that carried road and railway over the canal, past the branch that led down three locks to the River Dee and the big boatyard by the junction, and so out into the countryside again on their way to Ellesmere Port. It was a drab morning, grey and overcast, rain threatening in the dampness of the air, so that Jess was happy to leave Luke to complete the journey as he had expected to do the day before; he sat with Alice and Rosie in the stern well of the butty, talking and laughing while Annie Kain started on dinner in the cabin below. They had started out from Oldbury less than twenty-four hours after arriving there with the *Swan;* Mrs Kain had not had time to wash their clothes, and now Jess was aware that both of his working shirts, two of Luke's out-grown cast-offs, were getting rather smelly, so today he wore his best, in boater's parlance his 'stepping out' clothes. The smart check shirt that had been a present from his father, and the grey trousers that had once been his school wear.

At lunchtime as the clouds began to break they were tied at Ellesmere Port, above the Whitby Locks – but more bad news awaited them:

'Ain't no tug, mate. Gearbox is broke – won' be fixed terday, neither.' Abel Beechey was stuck there too, waiting for the tow down the ship canal to Stanlow and the oil refinery. He'd been there since the previous night: 'Ruddy pain in the backside! We won' get down 'til Monday now, you see if Oi ain't roight!'

'Why can't we go down on ar own? We've got engines in the boats, we could do it easy!' Jess was puzzled.

'They won' let oos, boy' Abel told him: 'They says as it's too dangerous, the Bolinders we got ain't powerful enough fer that. But Oi reckon it's 'cos they can charge oos fer the tow, get a few bob out of oos.'

'Whoyever it is, Jess, we'll 'ave ter wait, ain't nothin' we can do 'bout it.' Annie sounded a placatory note: 'Moight as well mek the best of it! Oi'll do the washin', Alice can pop ter the shops fer a few things. 'N Oi'm sure yeh'll want ter tek a leaf out o' Abel's book, eh?'

''Ow d'yeh mean, Ma?' She laughed:

''E'll be polishin' 'is h'injun! 'N now you got one ter play with too...' The two boys joined in her laughter:

'Per'aps we ortta get Moike Parker ter tek a look at it – just check it over, loike?' Luke suggested.

'Yeah, good idea' Jess concurred: 'I think I got it all fixed okay, but it'd be good ter make sure.'

'Yeh'll be loocky ter get 'old of 'im!' Abel warned them: 'E's got the tug gearbox in bits roight now.'

While Annie marshalled the two girls to go shopping, Jess and Luke strolled down to the lower basin and around to where the big tug bearing the legend 'Manchester Ship Canal' on its sides lay tied up, its engine covers gaping open. Stepping aboard, they found the engineer in that dark cavern of the engine-room, bending over the partly-dismantled gearbox. Sensing their presence, the overall-clad figure looked up:

'Hello Luke – how are you?'

'We're foine, Moike. 'Ow are yeh doin' wi' that?'

'Gettin' there. The bands on the cone are worn out, but they've got spares at the ship canal's stores. I'm waitin' for them to turn up at the moment.' He stretched his back, and climbed out to join them on the deck; he gave Jess a curious look:

'You must be Jess, right? The boy who saved little Rosie, a few weeks ago?'

'I guess so' Jess admitted; Parker laughed:

'You are or you're not, lad! It's a pleasure to meet you – that story's gone all round the Port. That was a very brave thing, to dive in out there.' Jess shrugged his shoulders:

'I didn' think about it. But I did think I wasn' goin' ter make it, fer a while!'

'Well, we're all proud of you anyway. Now – is there anythin' I can do for you, or are you just being curious?'

'We were wonderin' if yeh could tek a quick look at ar engine. The top seal went on the way 'ere – I fixed it, but it would be good ter 'ave yeh look at it, make sure it's okay.'

53

'Bolinder, is it?'

'Yeah. New'un.'

'Oh, right. They do that.'

'Yeah – s'the second one we've 'ad go.'

'Okay – tell you what: I can't do any more here until the parts turn up. I'll pop home for a bite of lunch, and then I'll come and take a look at your engine. Up the top, are you?'

'Yeah – The *Swan,* Clayton's motor. It's a new boat' Luke told him proudly.

'Right – I'll see you in a while, then!'

It was about an hour later that the tall figure in the well-used red overalls strolled up to where the *Swan* and the *Tove* lay against the bank above the paired locks. The day had turned out warm and sunny after the morning's clouds had dispersed, and a line of washing fluttered in the gentle breeze, the line strung from mast to cabin on the butty. Annie Kain was just hanging the boys' working shirts up to dry, and looked around as the engineer approached:

''Ello Moike! 'Ow are yeh?'

'Very well thank you, Annie. Yourselves?'

'Foine! Yeh coom ter tek a look at ar injun?'

'That's right – young Jess asked me to check it over after his repairs on the road.' Annie laughed:

'The two o' them's down there now, polishin' it! Bad as ar Abel they are now they got an injun ter play with!' She turned and called out:

'Luke! Jess! Mister Parker's 'ere for yeh!' They emerged from the engine-hole onto the bank:

54

'Thanks fer comin' Mister Parker' Jess greeted the man.

'No trouble, Jess. The parts for the tug'll be here any time, but I'll give yours a quick look-over while I can. Okay if I go down?'

'Sure, Moike' Luke assured him, and he climbed down into the boat.

'Roight, you two!' Annie addressed her boys: 'Get them shirts off! Moight as well wash 'em whoile Oi'm at it.'

'But ar other ones are still wet, Mam!' Luke protested.

'T'ain't cold terday, boy. You won' take any 'arm from a bit o' sunshoine!' Jess grinned at Luke, shrugging his shoulders; he peeled his best shirt off and handed it to her, and Luke, echoing his grin, followed suit. The two of them went to sit on the deck, but she further admonished them:

'These boats could do wi' a clean-oop – Luke, you sweep off the decks – Jess, get yerself a bucket o' water and mop down the cabins. Then there's the brasses as could do wi' shoining...'

'Yes Ma' they chorused, still grinning at each other. In truth, the boats already looked very smart, their fresh paint gleaming in the afternoon sunlight, the brasses already glittering, but the two boys set to with a will, their pride in their floating homes coming to the fore as Luke plied his broom and Jess his mop. Jess found himself as happy as he could ever remember, the sun warm on his bare back as he worked, the occasional splash of water from the mop only serving to make him feel even warmer, more comfortable. He washed down the butty cabin, then wiped it over with the mop wrung as dry as he could get it to prevent any marks being left as the water dried on the paintwork. He was about to start on the motor cabin when Parker emerged again from their engine-room, wiping his hands:

'It all looks fine, Jess. You did a good job there, lad.' Jess smiled at such praise:

'Thank yeh, Mister Parker!'

'Mike, Jess. No need for formality here! I've gone over the head bolts, given them an extra tightening – if you have to do that job again, remember to do that, the next day, it'll help stop the seal goin' again.'

'Oh – right, I will. Thanks.'

'What do we owe yeh?' Annie asked, looking up from her mangle; Parker chuckled:

'Forget it, Annie! It only took me those few minutes – you've got yourself a decent mechanic there, you'd best hang on to him!' She laughed:

'Oi intends ter, don' you woorry!' Parker turned to Jess again, held out his hand:

'Good work Jess. And the best of luck to you, lad.' Jess took the proffered hand:

'Thank yeh – Mike!' The man smiled at him:

'Now I'd better get back to that damned tug – I told them this would happen! One of their drivers is too gung-ho, slamming the gears from forward to reverse with the revs far too high, the clutches were bound to give out eventually. Maybe they'll listen now!'

'I hope so!' Jess recalled the wild ride down the ship canal they had taken before, that had resulted in

Rosie being thrown overboard. The engineer strolled away with a last wave over his shoulder, and Jess went back to his mop.

Chapter Eight

'Hello – have you seen my Dad?'

Jess was just emptying his bucket, Luke sweeping the pile of dust and twigs from the deck into the water, as a new voice sounded behind them. They looked around – a young boy stood there, a pair of red overalls tied by their arms around his waist, a blue shirt above them:

'Your Dad?' Luke queried.

'Yeah – Mum said he'd come to look at your engine.'

'Mister Parker, yeh mean?' Jess asked; the boy nodded:

'That's right, he's the engineer. I'm Reuben.'

''Is son?' The boy nodded. Jess grinned: 'And his assistant, eh?'

'Yeah – when I'm not at school!' Reuben grinned back: 'I'm going to be an engineer, as good as he is, when I'm old enough.'

'Good fer you! Pleased ter meet yeh, Reuben.' The boy stepped forward, a smile on his round, freckled face, and held his hand out – they shook:

'You too. You're Jess, aren't you? The boy who...'

'Dived in after Rosie! Yeah – but I'd rather people din't keep on about it.'

'Oh – okay.'

Luke stepped down off of the boats and shook his hand too:

'Yer Dad's gone back down ter the tug, in the bottom basin, mate. Yeh'll foind 'im there Oi 'spect. Oi'm Luke Kain, wi' Clayton's – these is ar boats.'

'They look really smart!' Reuben surveyed the gleaming pair.

'Thank yeh!'

'I'd better go and find Dad – see you later!' The boy turned away with a flick of his pale blond hair and ran towards the locks.

'You be careful!' Luke called after him, and got a quick grin back over his shoulder in reply.

Half an hour later the two of them were sitting talking, side by side on the deck of the butty. Annie Kain had run out of jobs to give them; she was just pegging out her last wash of the day, moving things along the line to make room to put their best shirts at one end. The rather uneven beat of an engine sounded from under Powell's Bridge, a hundred yards from where they sat, and they turned to look.

A tall skinny teenager stepped onto the bank from a pair of narrowboats and hurried towards them; the boats, riding high and empty, came on, the engine sounding distinctly rough. As they drew closer, Luke grimaced:

'It's 'Ampsons. Looks loike they didn' get no back-load from wherever they was goin'.' He sounded almost pleased at the idea. Jess, used by now to the usual camaraderie of the boating families, gave him a puzzled look:

'Yeh really don' like them, do you?' Luke shook his head:

'Nah. It's folks loike them what gets all boaters a bad name. You've seen 'ow some folks on the bank treat oos! Callin' oos dirty boaties – remember them kids in 'Ampton? 'N it's the loikes of Bert 'Ampson what gives 'em that idea.'

'Yeah – I see.' Jess felt vaguely disturbed at such conflict among the boating people – he had so far found only easy-going friendship evident among all the canal people he'd met.

The boy strode past them, barely acknowledging their existence or Jess's raised hand; the pair, looking as battered and unkempt as he remembered, swept past them and into the first of the wide locks that dropped into the lower basin, the man at the tiller dropping the tow and kicking the butty clear to run in alongside the motor. Quickly breasted, they descended into the chasm of the lock, and thence through the second to finally turn, still breasted up, into the lower basin. Jess and Luke had watched in silence, but now Luke commented:

''E'll be 'opin' fer a load o' clay. Oi'll bet that's what they've been on, clay ter Middlewich, when they passed oos th'other noight.'

The boys had wandered around to the high bank above the basin; now they stood looking down on the bustling activity below, boats and lighters being loaded and unloaded, cranes hissing and clanking, a small steam locomotive chuffing slowly along the narrow-gauge lines around the wharfside.

'Clay – is that what they 'ave down there?' Jess asked.

'All sorts o' stuff' Luke replied: 'Clay – china clay, fer the potteries – that's kep' in that shed there. Oop that end' he pointed to their left: 'thats's the raddle wharf where they keeps iron ore, what goes ter the iron works, even oop ter 'Ampton 'n Birnigum. They does a lot o' metal from 'ere too – copper 'n spelter 'n the loike. 'N food – flour 'n sugar. See them boats in the red 'n green, a bit loike ours? Them's Fellers's. They do most o' the carryin' out of 'ere, wi' Midland 'n Coast, them darker coloured boats, see?'

'Yeah - Fellows, Morton and Clayton...' Jess read off of the cabinside of a brightly-painted boat; he nodded: 'So they' he pointed to the scruffy boats that had just arrived: ''ave ter take what they can get, right?'

'S'roight. There ain't many number ones 'bout now, 'n they has ter get what loads they can. The decent ones does h'okay, get loaded in turn wi' the coomp'ny boats, but no-one loikes ter put loads on a rough pair loike 'Ampsons. 'E'll get mos'ly short trips loike Middlewich, prob'ly.'

'Number ones?' The expression had puzzled Jess; Luke laughed:

'S'what we calls men 'oo own their own boats! Ours 'ave numbers, roight, s'well as names - so do Fellers's 'n all the coomp'ny boats. But if yeh only 'as one pair o' boats, they've got ter be number one, right?'

''N now yeh call the men that too?' Luke nodded:

'Alwes 'ave doon.'

They strolled on together, down the steep slope of the bank to where the tug stood, its engine hatches still gaping open. Craning their necks to peer inside, they saw Parker in the process of reassembling the gearbox, his son at his side:

'The big spanner, Reuben – taa.' The boy handed him a long spanner, and Mike tightened the bolts holding down the gearbox cover. He'd sensed the presence of others, and glanced up:

'Hi, fellas! Come to see what's happenin'?'

'S'roight – 'ow're yeh gettin' on?' Luke affirmed.

'Nearly done. Just got to connect the propeller shaft, put some oil in and try it out.' He checked his watch: 'But you won't be getting down to Stanlow today, I'm afraid.' Luke shrugged:

'S'pose not. We'll 'ave ter wait 'til Monday now, Oi s'pose.'

'I imagine so. I'm sorry, Luke – I know lost time matters to you folk on the boats.'

'Yeah, well – can' be 'elped, can it? It'll be nice ter 'ave a rest!'

'You'll be okay for money?' The engineer understood the boaters' predicament, with no pay until the end of each trip.

'Yeah – Ma keeps a kind'a safety fund 'idden away. We won' starve!'

'I'm pleased to hear it!' Mike grinned up at him.

'Me too!' Jess's comment made them all laugh.

The boys watched as Reuben stood straddling the propeller shaft, holding it and rotating it a little way in each direction, easing it forwards until it met the flange at the back of the gearbox where his father helped him line it up accurately. They slipped the bolts through, spun the nuts into place and set about tightening them,

62

Mike on one end, his son holding the other with a second spanner. The job finished, they both stood back, stretching their backs with identical groans; Parker put an arm around his son's shoulders:

'Come on Reuben – time for a wash before tea!' Reuben smiled up at his father, and the two of them climbed out of the engine-room: 'We'll run this engine up an' try the gearbox in the mornin'. See you later, lads!'

'Yeah, see yeh, Moike. You too, Reuben.'

''Bye Luke, 'bye Jess.'

''Bye Reuben, Mike. Thanks for checkin' out ar engine.' Parker turned away with a wave, his arm still around Reuben's shoulders, and the two of them headed for home.

Chapter Nine

'Oi reckon Ma'll 'ave ar dinner 'bout ready by now.'
Luke turned and led the way back towards the upper
basin and their boats.

''Ope so – I'm starvin'!' Jess was more than ready
to follow him, despite the fascination of the bustling
activity all around him. They picked their way among
the men loading and unloading the boats and lighters,
and scrambled up the high bank to the upper level.
Crossing over the paired locks, one flight of wide ones,
the other narrow, they made their way back to where the
Swan and the *Tove* lay tied by the towpath above.

The line of washing still fluttered in the gentle
breeze above the butty's deck; Alice and Rosie sat on the
gunwales each side of the stern well:

'Jess! Luke! There you are!' Alice greeted them
with a smile.

'We've bin down ter see 'ow Moike's got on wi' the
tug' Luke told her: ''E's fixed it, but it's too late now,
they won' take oos down ter Stanlow 'til Monday.'

'What day is it terday?' Rosie asked.

'Friday!' Jess laughed – but he too had found it easy
to lose track of the days, travelling with the boats.

'So we got all weekend ter stay 'ere?'

'Yeah – two ruddy days wasted!' Luke sounded
annoyed at the reminder of their delay, but Rosie
chuckled:

'Tha's good!' Like any child, she relished the
chance to play with other kids her own age – not often
possible with her lifestyle.

'Yeh'll loike it when we runs out o' food 'cos Ma ain't got paid!' Luke grinned and aimed a playful clip at her ear, which she ducked, giggling:

'She won' let that 'appen!'

'Talkin' o' food – is dinner ready?' Jess's hunger prompted his question. Alice leant forward to peer in through the cabin doors:

'Joost coomin' oop!'

They all sat around in the early evening sunshine, plates on their laps, tucking in to a delicious pork casserole with gusto. A mug of tea washed it all down as they chatted, and then Abel and Sue Beechey wandered along, and the adults sat together talking – but not before Annie had issued her orders:

'Alice – do the washin' oop, will yeh? Rosie, you get the washin' in off the loine 'n sort it out, gi' the boys their'n ter put away.'

Luke and Jess sat with her and the Beecheys, listening in and adding the occasional comment or question to the conversation. Alice took the dishes and stood in the hatches, the hand-bowl steaming quietly in front of her as she gave them a good scrubbing, followed by the cooking-pots; Rosie went along the butty deck, taking down their clean clothes and collecting the clothes-pegs in their cloth bag. She sorted them into piles, and then handed one to Jess:

'There y'are Jess – them's yours.' A second pile went to Luke, and the rest she took down into the butty cabin. Jess idly looked through his pile; and a frown crossed his face:

65

'Rosie!' The girl's head popped up through the open hatch:

'What is it?'

''Ave yeh got me other shirt?'

'What shirt? Them's all there was on the loine.'

'Me best shirt! The one me Dad gave me, the check one.'

'Oh yeah, Oi know. It weren't there.'

'It must 'ave been! Ma just washed it, didn't you?' He turned to Annie, who nodded:

'Oi did – tha's whoy 'e 'n Luke ain't got no shirts on, 'cos I 'ad 'em off ter wash 'em.'

'Well where is it?' Jess was annoyed and upset – the smart shirt with its dark red, dark blue and white check was a reminder of his father. Rosie shrugged:

'Oi don' know Jess – Oi'm sorry! But it ain't there.'

'Could it 'ave blown away?' Alice looked up from her task, but Annie shook her head:

'Ain't bin no wind terday, not ter speak of. You sure it weren't there, Rosie?'

''Course Oi'm sure! Oi'd 'ave got it in else!'

Annie looked at the boy, aware of his distress:

'Only thing is, someone moost 'ave pinched it when we weren't lookin'. There's bin no end o' folks about terday. Oi'm sorry lad – but there ain't mooch we can do 'bout it.' Jess's shoulders slumped:

'I s'pose not. But keep yer eyes open, everyone, right? If yeh spots anyone wearin' it...'

A murmur of agreement ran around them, and Alice, her washing-up done, came and sat beside him, taking his hand in hers:

66

'Oi'm sorry, Jess. That was a lovely shirt; yeh did look good in it.' He gave her a smile:

'Yeah, thanks Alice. But it's 'cos me Dad gave it to me, really...'

'Oi know. Mebbe we can get yeh a new one, the same sort, loike.'

'Yeah, Mebbe. But it was expensive, I know – we can't afford that kind o' money. Oh well – it's only a shirt, really. I'll manage!'

Her smile was sympathetic as she squeezed his hand.

The conversation drifted on through the gathering darkness, but Jess took little part. He had had few possessions anyway, and he'd left most of them behind when he ran away from that awful foster-home in Smethwick. As a result, he was more upset than the simple loss of a shirt would seem to justify – but he had little enough of his own, and to be without that reminder of his father made his heart sink.

Chapter Ten

The disturbing feeling of loss was still with Jess as he got up the following morning. He was almost annoyed with himself – it was stupid, his rational mind told him, to get depressed because he'd lost a shirt. But it had been a link with that wonderful rogue who was his father, a man he loved and admired even though his drift into driving for the criminal classes had landed him in prison.

The day was dull and overcast, although quite warm, and they found themselves with little to do. He and Luke had done all the chores that Mrs Kain could find for them after arriving there the day before; they'd got their engine cleaned and polished to a state where it rivalled that of Abel Beechey, and now they were at a loose end. Rosie was happy enough, off playing with Abel and Suey's children, and those of the other boaters tied up at the Port awaiting orders; Annie had had a look of displeasure on her face when she'd spotted the grubby figure and worn dress of Maggie Hampson among them.

The boys wandered off, looking for something to hold their interest for a while; Alice ran after them and tagged along, linking her arm through Jess's with a proprietorial smile, which got her a grumpy look from her brother. Strolling around the lower basin, close to the clay shed, they spotted the *Constance* and the *Prudence,* sitting empty with no load offered, their open holds as much in need of cleaning as the rest of the boats. Enid Hampson stood in the butty's hatches, peeling potatoes and dropping them into a saucepan for their meal; there was no sign of her other children, but Bert could be heard banging around inside the motor's engine-hole. As they approached the boats, they saw Mike Parker coming from the opposite direction, accompanied by his smaller shadow.

'Hello Luke, Jess – you're looking very pretty today, Alice!' The engineer greeted them. The boys returned his greeting as Alice blushed pink, slipping her arm out of Jess's as Rueben grinned at her:

''Ello, Alice!'

''Ello Rueben. Yeh 'elpin' yer Dad terday?' The boy, his red overalls already looking somewhat oily, nodded:

'Yeah. We've got an engine to fix, in the *Ariel,* one o' Midland 'n Coast's motors. But Dad wants a word wi' Mister Hampson.'

The four children wandered a little way off as Mike stepped over the back-end plank of the *Prudence* at Enid's nod and knocked on the side of the *Constance.* They watched surreptitiously as Hampson's head appeared in the side-hatch, and an altercation began. It ended a few minutes later, with Hampson angrily snatching a battered old wallet from his pocket and handing over some money to Parker, who touched his forelock in ironic thanks. Rueben sniggered:

'Dad'll be happy! He's got paid for once.'

'Wha' do yeh mean?' Jess asked. Rueben flashed his cheeky grin again:

'Mister Hampson doesn't like paying up – Dad's had trouble with him before.'

'Why does 'e still work fer 'im then?' Rueben shrugged:

'He doesn't like to see boats standing doin' nothing, even if it's them, I suppose. The *Constance* needs a new engine, he says, or at least a full overhaul – but Mister Hampson won't pay for anything like that. Dad got it goin' again for him the other day, but he says it won't last long.'

'What'll 'e do when it breaks down agen?' Rueben laughed:

'Ask Dad to fix it again!'

'What if 'e can't? What if it's really broke next time, past fixin'?'

'Dunno. Maybe he'll have to get a job for one of the other firms, Fellows's or Midland. That's what his missus wants him to do anyway.'

''Ow do yeh know that?' Alice asked.

'I was talkin' to their Jimmie a week or two ago. He's a year younger than me, an' he's not as bad as the rest of them. I get on okay with Jimmie. Joe's a bit rough – he's the oldest, about your age Jess, but you'd best keep away from him. Jimmie says his Mum's fed up with strugglin' on their own, she thinks they'd be better off workin' for someone else. They'd probably get more loads that way.'

'And I s'pose the boats'd be looked arter for 'em?' Jess asked.

'That's right.'

'Come on Rueben, let's get to work!' Mike Parker walked up to them, a smile on his face; he put a hand on his son's shoulder and the boy looked up at him with a

70

grin on his face. The two of them strolled off with a backward wave, and Jess, Luke and Alice turned away, wandering towards the gate that led out into the town.

Just at the gate, they met the unkempt figure of Joe Hampson heading the other way, looking flushed and breathless, holding two loaves of bread under his arm. He returned Luke's curt nod as they passed, but then stopped and turned around:

'Hey!' They stopped and looked back.

'Yeh're Missus Kain's new kid are yeh? Wi' Claytons?' His eyes were fixed on Jess, who replied civilly even if he felt annoyed at the other boy's abruptness:

'S'right. Jess Carter.' He held out a hand, which Joe ignored:

'Ah. Moy Dad's a number one, right? We got ar own boats.'

'Pity 'e don' know 'ow ter look after 'em!' Luke snapped. Joe's face flushed angrily and he balled his free fist, but he restrained himself from lashing out, faced with the two of them:

'S'none o' your business 'ow we goes on! Yew leave oos alone, Luke Kain! Yew too, nigger-boy! Or yeh'll regret it.' He stormed off.

'Oh Jess! Don' listen ter 'im.' Alice looked distraught. Jess shrugged and gave her a smile:

'Don' worry Alice – I used ter get that all the time at school, I'm used to it. It don' mean nothin' – 'e can' 'elp bein' an ignorant beggar. But I see what Rueben meant about 'im! Nasty bit o'work, ain't 'e?'

'Teks after 'is old man' Luke said: "'E's a rough beggar 'n all, yeh don' want ter get on the wrong soide of 'im neither.'

'Come on, let's 'ave a look 'round the town 'n ferget them.' Alice urged them; they turned away and strolled out through the gates.

**

'There y'are Mam, coupl'a loaves for yeh.' Enid Hampson gave her eldest a withering look; but she took the bread he held out to her and disappeared with it down into her butty cabin. She reappeared moments later:

'Arsk yer Dad fer soom money Joe, 'n go 'n get soomat from the butcher. We'll 'ave no dinner ternoight else.'

"'E ain't got none, Mam. 'E's give it all ter Mister Parker.' Her second son's clean shirt was smeared with oil and grease as he climbed out of the engine-room of the motor boat.

'Jimmie! Look at the state o' that shirt Oi joost washed! What do yeh mean, 'e's give it all ter Moike?'

'Fer fixin' the h'injun.'

Enid's eyes turned skywards in despair as she gave a deep sigh:

'Oh well Oi s'pose 'e won' go boozin' it away oop the Tavern ternoight then. 'Old on Joe.' She vanished down into the cabin again, to reappear and hold out some coins to the boy: "'Ere's a coupl'a bob, see what yeh can get, Joe.' Her voice sounded resigned, almost hopeless.

'Yes Ma. Coom on Jimmie, we got things ter do.'

'Oh Joe! Do Oi 'ave ter?'

'Yes yeh do, or yeh'll get a belt! Now get movin'!'

'Not in that filthy shirt yeh don't!' his mother stopped him: 'Get it orf, 'n tek yer clean'un from the bed-'ole.'

Jimmie quickly whipped his shirt off over his head, not bothering to undo the buttons, and dived down into the motor cabin for his clean one. Joe had started walking to the dock gate, and the youngster had to run to catch up, pulling his shirt on as he went.

Chapter Eleven

Luke, Jess and Alice strolled out into Porter's Row, past the old dock-worker's cottages, and followed the main road as it curved away towards the railway line and the newer part of the town that lay beyond it. It wasn't often that they had the chance to explore like this; beyond the railway was new territory even for the two boater children who'd been through the Port so many times before. They knew the old canal town and its clustered narrow streets of terraced houses just beyond the dock gates, and the small shops there that would supply the needs of the boating community, but in the normal way their time at the Port would be restricted to the short delay waiting for the tug to take them to load; and once loaded, they would be returning to the Black Country as quickly as possible.

They had to wait at the level crossing for a local train to hiss and clank its way over the road; once across, they wandered along a narrow track behind the station from which they could watch the activity of the Wolverhampton Corrugated Iron Company's extensive factory. The clamour from the factory filled their ears, and little shunting engines hauled and pushed clusters of wagons around on the branch lines that ran into, out of and around the buildings. All the bustle fascinated Jess, even if Luke viewed it with a more jaundiced eye, aware that their own job was in competition with the railway – and Alice soon became bored, so they turned away and wandered on into the town itself, into the area known locally as Whitby.

Their exploration kept them occupied for an hour or more, before pangs of hunger made them think of returning to the boats:

'Mam was bakin' bread when we left – Oi wonder if it's done yet?' Alice speculated. The idea of hot crusty bread and butter, with slabs of tasty cheese, had all their stomachs rumbling.

They made their way back, crossing the railway line again but diverting along Westminster Road and into Church Street rather than following the main road all the way back. At the junction with Queen Street, Alice said:

'Let's go round the block – we can show Jess where the shops are!' The extra delay only adding to their anticipation of lunch, they turned left. Partway along, they passed the local bakers and two other shops in a little group together; the T-junction with Upper Mersey Street drew close as they walked on. Sounds of shouting greeted them as they got to the end of the street; and then a body hurtled around corner, almost cannoning into them in its haste. The shouting had resolved itself into yells of 'Stop – Stop Thief!'; Luke grabbed at the flying figure, but he wriggled free and ran on, along Queen Street the way the three of them had just come.

A police whistle joined in the noise from around the corner, and Jess took off in pursuit of the running fugitive. Slim and fit, he was soon on the other's heels; he launched himself forward in a rugby tackle, grabbing him around the knees. The two of them came crashing to the ground, and the other youth kicked at him, trying to get free; Jess hung on tightly, despite the other's

75

wriggling and kicking, and then Luke was there too, adding his weight and strength to the task.

Moments later, the rest of the pursuit caught up with them. A uniformed police constable took charge, hoisting their captive to his feet and quickly snapping a pair of handcuffs around his wrists. Jess bent to retrieve the package that the youth had dropped in the scuffle; he handed that too to the policeman, who showed it to the man who stood panting at his side:

'This what the boy stole, Mr Marsden?'

'That's right, Henry. Snatched it from the counter while I had my back turned. I was just cuttin' a bit of mutton for this other kid, when this'un grabbed Mrs Jones's best brisket and ran for it.' The copper gave the boy a hard shake:

'What's yer name, lad?' The boy didn't answer – but Luke had had time now to realise who they had caught:

''Ampson. Joe 'Ampson.'

'That right, boy?' Reluctantly, he nodded. 'Right. You're comin' to the station wi' me, lad. You two:' he turned to Jess and Luke: 'you come along too, I'll need to 'ave a statement from you 'bout what 'appened. You too, Mr Marsden.'

'Will it tek long? Only we ain't 'ad lunch.' Luke asked; the copper grinned at him:

''Alf an hour, maybe! And I reckon we can find you a cuppa tea ter keep yeh goin'.' Luke turned to Alice:

'Run 'ome 'n tell Mam what's 'appened, tell 'er we'll be back soon as we can.'

''Kay.' She looked admiringly at Jess: 'That were real brave of yeh, Jess, tacklin' 'im loike that! Oi'm so proud o' yeh!' She stretched up to plant a kiss on the surprised boy's cheek before dashing away.

'Well well, what have we here, Constable Petersen?' Sergeant Matt Whelan looked up from the front desk of the police station as the little group walked in.

'Our sneak thief, Sarge. These two boys caught 'im for us, stopped 'im red-'anded wi' this.' He placed the stolen brisket on the counter.

'He'd grabbed it from my shop, Matt. I'd got it wrapped ready for Mrs Jones from Nelson Road to pick up later, and I was serving this other young lad with a bit o' cheap mutton when this'un grabbed it and ran.' John Marsden added.

'And you two stopped him?' The sergeant spoke to Luke and Jess.

'Yeah. Jess caught 'im, 'n Oi 'elped 'old 'im down 'til the constable 'ere coom along.' Luke told him.

'Hmm. Well done, boys!' He turned back to Marsden: 'Where's this other kid, John?' Marsden thought for a moment:

'I don't know, Matt. He didn't follow us – he might be still at the shop, of course...' He paused, still thinking: 'I know him – not by name, but he's off the boats, I know that. Seen him before, plenty of times.'

'How old is he?' Whelan sounded suspicious.

''Bout ten or eleven, maybe.'

'Aah... You know him, boy?' He asked Joe.

'No! Course not.' But Joe's denial had been too quick, too emphatic, and Whelan gave him a long hard look.

'Right. Henry – lock young Hampson here in a cell, and I'll take statements from these boys and Mr Marsden. Is anyone looking after the shop, John?' The constable led his captive away as the butcher replied:

'The missus is there, Matt, she'll keep an eye on things.'

'Right.' He turned and called through to the back office: 'Frank! Get down to John Marsden's shop will you, talk to Mrs Marsden, see if she can add anything to what John's said, and find out if you can where this other lad's got to. I'd like to talk to him.'

A second constable emerged, putting his helmet on:

'Right, Sarge.'

'Then go over the Port, find that boy's family and tell them we've got him.'

'Right-oh.' He departed, striding off down the street, as Whelan ushered Luke, Jess and John Marsden through into the office.

Chapter Twelve

The sergeant swung three chairs to face the central desk in the office, and waved his guests to sit down:

'Okay – John, do you mind if I talk to these boys first? Let them get away for their lunch?'

'No, that's fine Matt, go ahead.' The butcher sat back, relaxing in his seat. Whelan turned to the two boys:

'You two – you're off the boats, are you?'

'S'roight' Luke told him: 'We're wi' Clayton's, the *Swan* 'n the *Tove.*'

'Moored in the Port, are you?'

'Yeah. Waitin' ter go ter load wi' h'oil.'

PC Henry Petersen returned from locking Joe in his cell, and the sergeant looked up:

'Brew us some tea, will you Henry?'

'Sure Sarge – four cups?' Four nods, and he disappeared again.

'Okay – can I take your names then, for a start?' Luke told him, and he jotted them down.

'Right – you actually stopped our thief, is that right?' Whelan asked Jess, who nodded:

'Yes – 'e ran past us, so I went arter 'im. I use'ter play rugby at school, so I tackled 'im, 'n then Luke 'ere 'elped ter 'old 'im until the policeman got there.'

'Okay – we're very grateful to you, young man. Now, can I get you to tell me that again, a bit more slowly, while I write it all down?'

Jess did as he was asked, letting the sergeant take it down as he told his story in more detail; their tea arrived while he was writing. At the end, Whelan read it through to him to confirm that he'd got it right, and then turned the form to him to sign at the bottom. He then started again with Luke, taking down his version of the events. With a second form filled in, he turned it to Luke and offered him the pen.

'Erm – sorry – Oi can' do that.' Whelan gave the boy a sympathetic look:

'Sorry lad, I should have thought. Can you just make a mark there, at the bottom?'

'Yeah – Oi can mek a letter L, will that do? That's moy initial – Abel showed me 'ow ter do that.' Whelan smiled at him:

'That'll do fine, Luke! Go ahead, lad.'

Luke signed the paper with a rather shaky L, and the sergeant added his full name beside it:

'Right – thank you, boys. And thank you again for stopping that lout – we've been after him for a while now! Now go on home and have your lunch, I'm sorry we've made you late for it.'

'Tha's all roight. What'll 'appen ter 'im now?'

'I'm not sure yet, Luke. Will you still be in the Port later?'

'Yeah – we're stoock 'ere 'til the tug teks oos down the h'oil dock on Monday.'

'Okay – I'll come by later and tell you what's happening. I take it you wouldn't want to be delayed here, to go to court and tell your story there?' Luke looked at Jess:

'Not if we can 'elp it! We don' get paid 'til we gets back ter h'unload – if we 'as ter 'ang around we're losin' money.'

'Right – I see... I'll come and see you later, all right?'

'Thanks. We can go now?' Whelan laughed:

'Yes! Go and get your lunch – and thank you again, both of you.'

***

In the Dock Street butcher's shop, PC Frank Hennesey was sipping at a cup of tea provided by his interviewee as she spoke to him:

'I was in the back, brewin' up for elevenses. I heard John yell, and came out to see what was up, just as he dashed out o' the door, so I didn't see anythin' o' what happened, not really Frank.'

'That's all right Joan. What about the other kid, the one John was serving when it happened?'

'Ah well – now he was lookin' scared when I came out there, and he headed for the door too. I yelled after him, didn't he want his meat, and he came back, lookin' kind o' sheepish, you know? He'd left it, and his money, on the counter – struck me as odd, but I suppose he was frightened.'

'You finished serving him?'

'Yes – took a shillin' off him for his bit o' mutton, 'cause I didn't know what John had cut for him, and that seemed about right.'

'He left then?'

'Yes – wandered out still lookin' scared, and went off towards the Port.'

'Boatee kid then, was he?'

'Reckon so, Frank. He's in here now and again, always got no money, lookin' for somethin' cheap. Don't know his name, I'm afraid.'

'Could he have been with the other boy? Keeping John busy so that he could grab something?' Joan Marsden shrugged:

'Could have been, Frank. Like I say, I didn't see anythin' until the other'un had done his runner. Would explain why he looked so scared, though!'

'Yew callin' moy son a thief?' Bert Hampson shaped up belligerently to the policeman, but Frank Hennesey stood his ground.

'He was caught red-handed, Mr Hampson. There's no question about it, I'm afraid.'

'Oi don' believe yeh! Moy kids ain't thieves, whatever yew say!' Hennesey shrugged his shoulders:

'You're welcome to come down the station and talk to my sergeant, Mr Hampson. We're holding Joe in a cell there, and you can see him as well, once he's been spoken to.' Hampson stared at him angrily, his fists still balled at his sides, but not daring to actually lash out at a uniformed constable. Enid, standing in the butty hatches, spoke up:

'Go down the station Bert, loike the man says, foind out what 'appened.' Her husband glanced at her, his expression still furious, but he kept himself in check. Turning back to the policeman, he drew a deep breath:

82

'Tell your sergeant Oi'll be there roight away, 'n Oi wants ter talk ter moy boy.'

'I'll tell him, Mr Hampson.' Hennesey looked at Enid:

'You have other children, Mrs Hampson?'

'Oi do, h'officer.'

'Are they here?'

'No, they're off playin' wi the h'other kiddies.'

'Do you have another son, a younger boy?'

'Oi've got two o' them.' She was regarding him suspiciously now.

'One of them be about ten or eleven, by any chance?' She hesitated, but then replied:

'Jimmie's ten. Whoy?' But Hennesey turned to Bert:

'Would you please bring young Jimmie with you to the station, Mr Hampson? We'd like to talk to him.'

'Whoy's that?' Hampson glowered at him.

'There was a younger boy in the shop at the time. We'd just like to eliminate Jimmie, make sure it wasn't him, you understand?'

'Jimmie's been 'ere all mornin'! Ain't 'e, Ma?'

'S'roight Bert.'

'But you don't know where he is now?' Neither answered the constable's question. 'Don't forget to bring him with you, Mr Hampson.' He saluted the boatman, nodded to Enid and walked away.

Chapter Thirteen

Luke seemed unusually thoughtful as the boys made their way back through the town again towards the docks. After a while, Jess asked him:

'What's up Luke? Yeh're very quiet.'

'Oh, s'nothin'.' Jess frowned at his friend:

'Come on Luke! What is it?'

'Well – it's joost – Oi ain't sure if we done the roight thing.'

'Wha'd'yeh mean?'

'Well – they may be a bunch o' rodneys, but 'Ampson's is still boaters. Oi'm not sure as we should'a 'anded Joe over ter the cops loike that.'

'What? We caught 'im thievin'! What else could we 'ave done?' Luke shrugged:

'Yeah, s'roight, Oi s'pose. But it joost don' feel roight, givin' 'im ter the cops.' Jess stared at him for a few steps, seeing the worried look on his face, but then he said:

'Yeah... I think I see. Like when they was lookin' fer me, 'n you didn't let on I was with yeh in the boat?'

'Yeah, kind'a. Loike Oi said teh yeh then, we don' 'elp the 'thorities on the bank if we can 'elp it. They don' 'elp oos, call oos dirty boatees 'n mek loife difficult fer oos. So mebbe we should'a let 'im go.' Jess thought for a moment:

'But you said as it's folks like them as gets all boatees a bad name! If we catch 'im 'n 'and 'im over, it's like – puttin' that right, a bit, ain't it? Fer the honour

84

o' decent boatees, right?' Luke looked at him and grinned:

'Yeah, Oi s'pose so! 'N part o' me thinks 'e's got what 'e deserves any'ow. D'yeh thnk they'll send 'im ter prison?' It was Jess's turn to shrug:

'Dunno, prob'ly. Serve 'im right, nasty beggar!'

They walked back in through the dock gates in a rather more cheerful mood, and made their way back up to the top basin and their boats. Alice saw them coming, and dashed up to them, giving her brother a quick hug and then throwing her arms around Jess. She stretched up to kiss his cheek, but he turned his head as she did so and their lips met. She jumped back, turning scarlet, and he looked embarrassed too:

'Oh! Sorry, Alice, I didn' mean that...' But she gave him a shy smile that only made him grin back at her.

Annie spoke from the butty hatches:

'Yeh're back then, boys? Oi'm afraid the bread's got cold, but it's noice 'n fresh, 'n Rosie's been ter the shops 'n got oos some nice fresh butter 'n a bit o' decent cheese.'

'Oh, thanks Mam! Oi'm starvin'!' Luke sounded relieved, and Jess concurred:

'Yeah, me too Mam! Thanks.'

'Cuppa tea ter wash it down? Or would yeh loike some lemonade fer a change?'

'Oh yeah! Tha's great, Mam, thanks!' Jess was relishing a cold drink on such a warm day, but Luke looked doubtful:

'Can we afford that, Mam? We ain't goin' ter get loaded 'til Monday.'

'Yeah, course we can!' Annie sounded dismissive: 'Yeh knows Oi keeps a bit back, joost in case. Any'ow, we got ter celebrate yer catchin' that thief, ain't we?' Now Luke nodded:

'Yeah – roight!'

'I wish as I 'ad some money, ter 'elp out' Jess said; Annie turned to him, puzzled:

'Whoy would yeh want ter do that, Jess? We earns enough fer all of oos.'

'Well – yeh've done so much fer me. Lookin' arter me, feedin' me 'n givin me clothes 'n all that...'

'What else would we do, boy? Yeh're part o' the fam'ly now! You ain't 'ad no more than Oi'd'a give ter Luke or the girls.'

''N look what yeh've done fer oos, Jess.' Alice's shy voice chipped in: 'It'd be 'ard ter run two boats without yeh – 'n yeh fixed the h'injun t'other day. We couldn'a done that.' Jess smiled at her, thinking to himself that they would really have managed the pair quite well on their own – but he said nothing, grateful for her words. Annie looked carefully at him:

'Wha's brought this on all of a sudden, lad?' Jess found it hard to describe how he was feeling:

'Well – I think, mebbe, it's 'cause of seein' Joe in 'andcuffs, 'n gettin' put in a cell. I mean – if I 'adn't met you, I'd prob'ly still be livin' on the streets, 'n mebbe 'avin' ter steal food fer meself. I mean, it could'a been me gettin' locked up, if it weren't fer you...'

'Oh, Jess! Coom 'ere boy!' She stepped over onto the dockside and held her arms out to him, and he let himself be drawn into her ample embrace: 'Ain't nothin' loike that goin' ter 'appen ter you now – yeh're one o' moine, Jess, 'n safe as safe can be.'

'S'roight Jess, yeh're one of oos now!' Alice came and slipped her arm through his as her mother let him go. Annie gave him a big grin:

'Loike Oi said Jess, ain't nothin' bad goin' ter 'appen ter you now. Not unless Oi catch yeh kissin' moy daughter agen, any'ow!' Alice turned bright red again, and Jess had the grace to look sheepish – but moments later they were all roaring with laughter.

After a delicious lunch, washed down with the promised lemonade, the boys moved the *Swan* across the basin to fill its fuel tank with diesel oil. In their absence, Annie took the opportunity to soak and scrub many of the lengths of rope normally used in running the boats, cleaning them of the grease and grime that inevitably adhered to them in the course of their work. As she bent over the washtub, a cough sounded behind her, and she looked around:

'Oh – Sergeant! Was yeh lookin' fer oos?' Matt Whelan removed his helmet with a smile:

'Your two boys, Ma'am. I promised to let them know what was going to happen to the lad they caught for us this morning.'

'Ah – can yeh 'ang on fer a minute? They're over there' she gestured across the basin: 'gettin' topped oop wi' gas-oil fer the h'injun. They won' be long.'

'Yes, of course. You're Mrs Kain, Luke's mother?'

'S'roight. This is Alice, moy daughter' she indicated the girl helping her: ''N Rosie, moy youngest, she's off playin' wi' the h'other kiddies soomwhere.'

'And you've adopted young Jess, the coloured lad?' She chuckled:

'We found 'im sleepin' rough, in Birnigum. Couldn' leave 'im there, could Oi?' Whelan smiled again:

'No, indeed. He's a nice kid – so's your Luke. You must be proud of the pair of them?'

'Oh ah! They're good boys, on the 'ole.'

Matt stood back to let her get on with what she was doing, and watched as the two teenagers manoeuvred the long boat back across the basin, shunting back and forward, Luke wielding the long shaft from the front deck while Jess worked the engine. They were soon tying up alongside the *Tove;* both had spotted the policeman waiting for them, and quickly stepped across to the dockside once the boat was secured.

''Ello Sergeant.' Jess greeted him with a smile; Luke was rather more reserved, merely nodding cautiously.

'Hello again, boys. I've come to tell you what's happening.'

'Would yeh loike a cuppa tea?' Annie interrupted, wiping her hands on her apron, and Whelan looked around:

'I'd love one, Mrs Kain! Thank you.' She chuckled again:

'Coomin' oop!' She disappeared down into the butty cabin, and Whelan turned back to the boys.

'Is Joe goin' ter prison then?' Jess asked before he could say anything. He shook his head:

'Not this time, Jess.' He smiled at the boy's surprised expression: 'I know you two caught him red-handed, stealing that meat from John Marsden's shop, and we all know he's been stealing from shops around here – and elsewhere, probably – for months now. But it's a question of what I could prove in court, you see. He claims that he's never stolen anything before, and that he only did it now because they haven't got any money, and he wanted to get something for them to eat. It seems his father had to pay all the money he had for repairs to their boat's engine, and they hadn't any left for food.'

'Do yeh believe that?' Luke sounded scandalised: 'No-one on the cut would take a man's last penny 'n leave 'em wi' no food! 'N sensible folks keeps a bit fer h'emergencies – moy Mam does, any'ow!' Whelan put his hands up with a smile to ward off his anger:

'I know, Luke! But that's what he's saying, and it's the kind of sob story that's likely to make the magistrates take pity on him and let him off with a slapped wrist. I can't prove any of the other thefts were his doing, because no-one's ever got a good enough look at him to identify him for certain.'

'So 'e's goin' ter get orf with it?' Jess asked.

'Oh no!' Whelan chuckled: I'm keeping him in the cells tonight, and then I'll let him go tomorrow, with an official police caution. That will go on the record – and if he's ever caught stealing again, they'll know about that caution, and it'll go against him in court, you see. So I'm hoping he'll learn his lesson, and keep his hands to himself in future.'

Annie reappeared with two mugs of tea. Whelan took his gratefully, and sat on the edge of the butty's deck next to her as she waved an invitation. He took a sip, and looked up at the boys again:

'I've had a word or two with his father, and his younger brother, as well. The youngster was in the shop too, buying a bit of cheap mutton for his mother – yes, I know that tends to give the lie to Joe's story, but he says he didn't know about that. I think he deliberately took advantage of that distraction to snatch the piece of brisket, but again I can't prove it. But I've put the fear of his life into young Jimmie, who seems like a different kid altogether from his brother, so I don't think he'll let himself get sucked into any more of Joe's shenanigans in the future.

'And I should warn you both – I've told their father that I will be keeping an eye on him as well. He was shouting his mouth off about you two letting the boaters down, getting his kids into trouble, and I've warned him to keep his mouth shut and not to talk to you or approach you about it. But I'd advise you to keep well away from him yourselves.'

'Don't worry, we don' want anythin' ter do wi' them.' Luke assured him; Annie laughed:

'Oi can 'andle the loikes o' Bert 'Ampson! 'E's a ruddy coward, loike all bullies, if anyone stands oop ter 'im.'

90

'Still, I'd suggest you be careful around him, all of you.'

'Bloomin' rodneys, all of 'em!' Whelan looked up at Luke's angry tone:

'Rodneys?' Annie laughed again:

'S'a boater's h'expression, sergeant! It means folks as don' look after 'emselves or their boats in a proper fashion. Yeh've seen the state o' them boats o' their'n?'

'I have! Nothing like yours, Mrs Kain, these two look very smart indeed.'

'Ah well, we keeps 'em that way. So do all *proper* boaters – not loike them as we call rodneys, yeh see.' Whelan laughed out loud now:

'I've got a brother called Rodney! You wait 'til I tell him that!'

'Oh – we don' mean no disrespect teh no-one...'

'I know that, Mrs Kain – but I can have a laugh at his expense, can't I?'

Chapter Fourteen

With the police sergeant gone back to his duties, Annie carried on with her own tasks. Alice, in her oldest clothes, sat cross-legged scrubbing at the wet ropes; Luke and Jess promptly disappeared into the engine-hole, rags in hand, and set about wiping down the engine and polishing its assorted brass and copper fittings. But they were to have another visitor...

A little later, as Alice and her mother were stretching out the newly-cleaned ropes along the length of the boats to dry in the sun, a man approached them with a package under his arm. Alice, recognising him, greeted him with a smile which he returned as he approached Annie:

'Excuse me – are you Mrs Kain?' Annie turned around, stretching her back:

'Oi am; what can Oi do for yeh?'

'You're Luke's mother? And young Jess's...' She laughed:

'Oi'm pretty mooch 'is Mam too, Oi reckon! Fer now, any'ow.'

'Are the boys around?'

'They went off a little whoile ago' Alice offered: 'Oi don' know where they was goin'.'

'Oh – well, never mind. Here, Mrs Kain, this is for you and your family.' She took the proffered package, a puzzled look on her face, and carefully unwrapped it:

'Oh! Oh, we can't tek this! It's real noice o' yeh, but...'

'Please, Mrs Kain? It's just a small thank-you for what your boys did today. That thieving lout had been stealing from the shops here for ages, and we're all grateful that he's been stopped. So I'd like you to have that as a token of our thanks.'

'Oh... Well, Oi don' know as Oi should...'

'Please? It's just a piece of decent top-side of beef and few sausages – enjoy them, with our gratitude.'

'Well, if yeh puts it loike that... Thank yeh, Mister..?'

'Marsden, John Marsden. I've got the butcher's shop in Dock Street.'

'Yes, of course! Sorry, Oi didn' reconoise yeh out o' the shop, without yer apron! Thank yeh very mooch, Mister Marsden.'

He turned away with a nod of the head and a smile for Alice.

'Well, Gal!' Annie looked at her daughter, rubbing her hands in delight: 'We shall eat well fer the next few days! Go 'n put these in the cold-hole – we'll 'ave boiled beef 'n carrots tomorrer, 'n the sausages should keep fer the day after.'

'What's fer tonoight, Mam?'

'Oi did enough o' the mutton stew yesterday to do today 'n all, so we'll finish that off. Wi' some chips from the shop – 'ow's that?' Alice grinned her approval as she took the re-wrapped meat and placed it in the small cupboard below the step in the butty cabin. Set into the stern of the boat and cooled by the surrounding water, that served as the boaters' 'refrigerator', keeping meat and milk surprisingly cool and fresh even in the hottest weather.

***

The rest of the weekend passed without incident. Sunday dawned warm and sunny, and they all enjoyed the continuing fine weather – until a series of thunderstorms blew in up the estuary to dump their anger on the rising ground around Ellesmere Port. Such bad weather held little fear for the hardy boating people, used to having to work in all conditions; Luke had a chuckle at Jess's expense when the younger boy dived for cover as the first storm struck. He soon emerged again, smiling ruefully, his coat on, his flat cap crammed down on his head.

The two spent some time sitting around behind the tall warehouses of the Port, watching the big ships passing by on the Manchester Ship Canal. Luke muttered darkly about them being able to continue to work while their boats were held immobile by the lack of the tug, grumbling at the delay, but he brightened up when Jess reminded him about the treat awaiting them, the delicious piece of beef cooking on the range and the jacket potatoes in the oven. And prompted by Jess, he cheered up even more in retelling stories of his childhood, horse-boating when his father was still alive, laughing about times he had fallen in the canal and been fished out by his hair and rescuing Alice as a toddler when she'd been trapped against a fence by Mabel, their old and rather grumpy horse.

94

In their wanderings, they refrained from going down to the lower basin in order to avoid a confrontation with the Hampsons. But they were, by chance, looking down from the high bank above it when a uniformed PC escorted a rather chastened-looking Joe back in through the gates and delivered him back to the *Constance*. Hampson senior emerged to meet them, and what was obviously an angry altercation took place with the policeman, who eventually left with an ironic salute to the boatman, having kept his cool throughout. Joe disappeared into the motor cabin, and they saw no more of him.

The boiled beef was as delicious as expected, slow-cooked over carrots and onions on the range, and accompanied by crispy-skinned jacket potatoes. And afterwards, Annie dipped a little further into her emergency fund, and they strolled along the towpath, past the football ground, to the Canal Tavern by the next bridge, where she enjoyed a glass of stout while the girls and Jess had lemonade. The landlord raised an eyebrow but didn't demur when she ordered a half-pint of shandy for Luke, unsure just how old the stocky, weather-beaten youth might be. A last mug of tea, and an early night to be up in time to work the boats down the locks in the morning, ready for the tow out to Stanlow to load.

Chapter Fifteen

Awoken by some kind of instinctive mental alarm clock, Luke was up and about at first light on the Monday morning. Jess, after a weekend getting used to the more relaxed regime while they awaited the tug, turned over with a groan as his friend's movements disturbed him; Luke chuckled:

'Coom on Jess, toime ter be oop! Back ter work, mate.'

'Yeah, okay!' Jess rolled onto his back and sat up as Luke slid the hatch back and emerged into the grey dawn.

By the time he too climbed out of the cabin, a steaming mug of tea awaited him on the cabin-top, and he sipped at it gratefully. Luke was already down in the engine-hole, firing up the blow-lamp to preheat the Bolinder engine and pumping up fuel into the day-tank ready to work the pair down the locks. Activity bustled around the other pairs of Clayton boats queued above the locks – a number of pairs had accumulated during the days while the tug had been out of action, and then over the weekend itself. In front of them, Abel Beechey already had his engine running, and Jess returned his cheery wave as he clambered out of his engine-room. The older boatman strolled back along the bank:

'Mornin' Jess! Yeh ready ter go?'

'Yeah – Luke's startin' the engine.'

'Ah. Two pairs in front of oos – tug'll only tek three at once, so there's not the roosh fer you ter get down. But yeh'll be front o' the queue fer the next tow!'

'Right – thanks, Mister Beechey. Yeh 'eard that, Luke?' A head appeared at the engine-hole doors:

'Yeah – cheers, Abel! We'll tek ar toime – give Jess 'ere a chance ter wake oop!' Jess aimed a playful swipe at Luke's head and he ducked, laughing. Alice, standing in the butty's hatches with her own mug of tea, looked on with a happy smile.

'Yeh 'ad a ter-do wi' 'Ampsons th'other day?' Beechey asked.

'Jess caught Joe, stealin' from Mister Marsden's shop!' Alice piped up.

'That's what Oi'd 'eard! You be careful there, boy, 'Ampson's a rough'un, 'n Joe ain't mooch better.' Jess shrugged:

'We'll be away from 'ere terday.'

'Yeah, but 'Ampson's likely ter 'old a grudge. Watch out when yeh gets back 'ere agen, both o' yeh.' The rattle of paddles sounded from the top lock, and Beechey looked around: 'Ar turn ter go – see yeh later, fellas.'

Luke stepped back down to the engine and checked the blow-lamp. With the cylinder-head plug glowing red-hot, he set the throttle and bent to the flywheel, turned it to the compression point and stepped heavily on the sprung pin. As usual, the big engine turned over slowly under his weight; the loud report sounded up the exhaust-pipe as it fired, spun over faster, fired again, and settled to its steady rhythm. Around them, the sound of a number of Bolinders echoed from the old warehouses as other pairs prepared for the new day's work.

Abel Beechey ran his boats into the top lock, set ready by his wife and children, and Luke eased the *Swan* and the *Tove* forward, still breasted up side by side, as Jess and Alice untied them from the dockside. With a delay waiting for them while the tug returned from the Stanlow oil dock, they didn't hurry working down the two locks, and then down the third at the side of the central island in the lower basin. Between, they passed the *Constance* and the *Prudence,* tied near the clay shed. Bert Hampson stood in the hatches of his butty with a mug of tea; he gave them a glare as they emerged from the second lock but disappeared down into the cabin without a word, much to Jess's relief. As they worked through the last lock, he noticed a man in a bowler hat stride up to the dirty, scarred boats and knock on the cabinside – but then they were going down, and he hurried to open the gates for Luke.

Minutes later, a second pair of Clayton boats joined them – Steve Dulson, still bucking the trend and the company's wishes and running his old pair of horse-drawn boats, his grandchildren providing the crew. And then the tug was back, hitching both pairs on, and setting off again out onto the wide waters of the Ship Canal.

***

In the lower basin, Bert Hampson emerged again from his cabin at the knock on its side:

'Yeah?'

'Steerer 'Ampson, we've got a load for yeh. Iron ore, fer Wolver'ampton.'

'Oh ah? 'Ow mooch?'

'It'll be about thirty tons, mebbe a bit more.'

'Thirty ton? That ain't 'ardly worth loadin'!' The man shrugged:

'It's the last of a batch ter go. Fellers's 'ave put two pair 'n two single motors on, but that's all the boats they got available. This'll be subbed from them, if yeh wants it.' Hampson stared at him, but then he nodded grudgingly:

'Yeah, all roight, if that's all yeh got fer oos. Ruddy 'alf-load!'

'Too much fer a single – I'll try 'n 'old back a bit more, so yeh gets a decent payout, all right?'

'Yeah, h'okay. Thanks.' The last word again came out reluctantly.

'Right. Get down ter the Raddle Wharf, soon as yer like, the last o' the Fellers's boat are loadin' now.'

The man strode off, and Hampson climbed down to start his engine. Unlike a Bolinder, the two-cylinder Russell Newbery needed no pre-heating; but the tired, worn-out engine of the *Constance* was a reluctant starter at best. It took him many minutes of cursing and swearing, cranking the engine over, before it eventually fired, releasing a dense cloud of heavy grey smoke as it rattled unhappily into life.

He and Joe eased the pair past the clay shed to the far end of the basin and the extensive wharf where assorted cargoes of metals and ores were stored and loaded. As they singled out, ready to tie against the dockside for loading, two single motor boats with the name 'Fellows Morton & Clayton Ltd' emblazoned on

99

their cabinsides pulled away, passing them on their way to the locks and the road South. They tied beside the wharf, below a row of battered-looking railway wagons, and the foreman came over:

'Yeh've got thirty-four ton seven 'undredweight ter load. Where d'yeh want it?'

''Bout twenny-four ton in the butty, the rest in the motor.' Hampson still sounded disgruntled at the short load, and the foreman gave him a frown:

'Yeh don' 'ave ter tek it yeh know!'

'Oi'll 'ave it – but short load means short money. We could tek another twenny ton, yeh knows that!' The foreman shrugged; but he had some sympathy with the boatman:

'Yeah, I know mate. But it's all we got.' He waved to the men on the wagons, calling them forward, and soon the loose ore was clattering down from the tipping wagons into the holds. Joe and his father wielded shovels to get it spread out so that the boats would lay on an even keel, balanced for the journey. An hour later, they were away again; the foreman watched them go with a shake of the head. One of his men, standing at his side leaning on his shovel, muttered:

'What kind o' boater is that, who don't even stop ter mop the dust off'n the boats 'fore they go?' The foreman grimaced:

'Fellers's only use 'em if they're desp'rate. There weren't no-one else available.'

'Hnh!'

Chapter Sixteen

Jess was pleased that their trip behind the tug on the Ship Canal was rather less spectacular than his last experience of it. They had a different tug driver, a cheerful-looking grey-haired man with a quick smile under his flat cap, who took them at a more stately pace, leaving them tied at the oil wharf to await their turn to load. The hoses were pouring the fuel oil into the second of the three pairs already there; once the third pair was loaded, the tug picked up all six boats and turned with them back in the direction of the basins of Ellesmere Port.

Then it was their turn – the hoses were dropped in through the open hatches in the boats' decks, and the oil began to gurgle into the holds. Loading didn't take very long – around mid-morning they were ready to go, the boats now sitting deep in the water, their hatches closed and sealed. But they had to wait for Steve Dulson's boats to be loaded too before the tug would take them back to the Port. While they waited, Luke and Jess spent half an hour getting the engine started so that they would be ready to go as soon as they were back; then a quick mug of tea and some bread and butter before the tug swung into place and dropped its towlines over their front T-studs. With the two horse-boats tied on behind them, they were soon back, setting off up the three wide locks of Ellesmere Port just after midday.

***

One hour and several miles in front of the *Swan* and the *Tove,* a vague trail of bluish smoke marked the passage of the *Constance* and the *Prudence.* The tired, dirty motor boat sat level in the water, part-loaded, deep enough to give its propeller a good grip but still riding relatively high; behind it, the grubby butty floated deep-down, seventy feet away on its long towline, Enid Hampson leaning on the tiller as she peeled potatoes for the day's meal.

Bert was steering the motor, Joe standing on the gunwale next to him; the two youngest chidren played in the hold, on top of the light load of crushed iron ore, but Jimmie rode with his mother on the butty, feeling far from happy. The interview with the police sergeant two days before had seriously shaken him, despite his father's upbeat judgement on the situation – 'yeh're all roight boy, they can' prove nothin'!'. He loved his father – but he was old enough to know that he was not perhaps the most upright of citizens, nor the best-regarded by his peers. And he'd been getting increasingly unhappy at being drawn into Joe's thieving exploits, being made an accessory to his petty crimes. Now, sitting morosely beside his mother, he made up his mind to stand up for himself, to say no to Joe next time, even if he did get a belting for it.

The day had dawned fine and clear, but later, as the afternoon drew on, cloud began to gather in the west and roll towards them, eventually dampening them all with a steady drizzle. Evening saw them well beyond Chester, past Northgate Staircase and the five separate locks that raised them onto the Cheshire plains and driving along the eight-mile pound towards Wharton Lock. The old, tired Russell Newbery engine was flat out – but even Bert had to admit to himself that it wasn't running properly. Down on power, smoking badly, they were losing time where they should be making a good speed on the open channel of the wide Chester Canal.

***

''Oo's that in front?' Jess peered ahead. Luke, on the tiller at his side, frowned:

'Oi reckon it's ruddy 'Ampsons! Looks loike their grubby boats. They must'a got a load whoile we was out ter Stanlow.'

'We catchin' 'em up?'

'Yeah. 'Is h'injun's about 'ad it; remember what Reuben said? 'N we got a brand new'un!' he added proudly. Jess shared a grin with him:

'Can we go past 'em?'

'If 'e'll let oos. Most boaters'll loose yeh by if yeh're goin' faster'n them, but Oi wouldn' trust 'im ter do that.'

And as Luke had guessed, the boats in front showed no inclination to move aside and let them past as they drew ever closer behind. They saw Hampson look back several times, to see them following, but each time he resolutely looked to his front again, ignoring their presence. Overtaking on the canal is not easy at best, so they had no choice but to slow down and remain behind; hearing the beat of the Bolinder slow, Annie strode forward to stand on the butty's fore-deck. She called out to them, asking what was happening; Luke turned and called back:

'We caught oop wi' 'Ampsons – they're goin' slow but 'e won' loose oos past!' She thought for a moment, looking around at the gathering dusk:

''S'gettin' late – let's tie at the old wharf by the Royal Oak. 'Ampson'll go late, so 'e'll be out of ar way in the mornin', then we can 'ope 'e's fer Middlewich agen so 'e'll turn off at Barbridge.'

'Roight-oh Mam!'

An hour later, Luke let the boats slow as they passed under Bate's Mill Bridge. The butty ran up alongside, between the motor and the bank, and they quickly tied them side by side before mooring on the disused wharfside. Bert Hampson glanced behind, hearing the Bolinder drop back to tickover above the rattle of his own engine, and gave a self-satisfied smile as he saw them stopping.

'We goin' ter the pub agen Mam?' Annie chuckled:

'Not ternoight Luke! Oi've dipped inter moy 'mergency fund already, 'n Oi ain't spendin' more of it joost 'cause you want a shandy – yeh'll mek do wi' tea, lad!'

104

Chapter Seventeen

Up with the dawn as usual, Luke and Jess had the Bolinder running almost before Annie had brewed the tea the next morning – today Jess was in charge, steering the *Swan,* and he was under way, mug in hand, bread and cheese on a plate before him on the slide, while Luke set off on the bike to prepare their first lock.

Jess was feeling proud and nervous at the same time – today he would have to take the pair of boats into the locks with a full load on for the first time. He'd found it quite easy with the empty butty right behind him on the cross-straps, but now it was eighty feet away, swimming independently on its long tow-line, and he'd have to judge it just right so that it would come up alongside him as he stopped the motor, coiling in the rope at the same time so that it didn't get caught up around the propeller. Too fast, and it would fly past him and hit the far gates – too slow, and it would stop before coming fully into the lock. And either way he would feel Luke's unspoken scorn at his ineptitude, even if the older boy would tactfully keep his silence.

Ten minutes later, Wharton Lock appeared in front of him through its adjacent bridge, the gates standing open. He let the *Swan* lose speed gradually, copying what he'd seen Luke do the day before. Under the bridge, and he pulled the clutch out; now the *Tove* began to catch him up, carried by its momentum, and he bent to take the line from the dolly behind him and began to coil it in. He let the boat drift on into the lock, deliberately taking his time; the butty was almost alongside him now, steered into the gap by Alice, and he dropped the towline onto its foredeck, and then turned to his controls. Quickly reversing the engine, pushing the clutch in again to brake the *Swan* to a halt, he picked up the short, heavy rope from the *Tove's* cabintop and dropped it over his stern dolly. Attached to its anser-pin on the butty's stern, the rope snapped tight, drawing the two boats together and stopping the butty's forward motion; looking up, he saw that he'd got it just about right. The boats sat side by side in the lock, just short of hitting the top gates in front of him.

The sound of clapping from beside him, and he glanced back with a grin for Alice as she applauded him. On the lockside above, Annie and Luke had the bottom gates closed; and then water was frothing in through the top paddles as the boats began to rise. In a matter of moments, they were on their way again; a mile further on, and they worked through the two Beeston locks; then the single lock at Tilstone, soon followed by the two-lock staircase of Bunbury. Here Jess threw his stern rope across the butty's T-stud and drew it tight while Luke did the same at the bows, tying the boats together so that he could drive forward into the second lock. Clearing Bunbury, they faced the nine-mile pound to Hack Green locks which would take them past the junctions at Barbridge and Hurleston.

The day had started fine, but now cloud was drifting across from the west, throwing a sudden chill over them until the sun reappeared. As they passed the junction where the Middlewich branch turned off, Luke peered under the bridge in the hope of seeing Hampson's pair heading away from the main line of the canal, but he was disappointed. He couldn't see very far in that direction, and hoped that they were perhaps long gone. Fifteen minutes later they passed the turn that led onto the Welsh canal to Llangollen; and then a series of sweeping bends saw them approaching the town of Nantwich. Past the turn into Nantwich Basin, under the big white bridge there, around a tight right-hand bend and over the aqueduct, out onto the long embankment.

Half an hour later, the two locks of Hack Green drew slowly closer in front of him, and Jess's nerves returned with new force. These would be his first narrow locks with the boats loaded – the first time for all of them to work a heavy pair of boats uphill singly, in fact. Abel Beechey had spoken of 'long-lining' the boats through, but Jess for one had only the dimmest idea of what that meant; he hoped that Luke knew how to go about it, and would keep him right; but his friend had jumped off again at the last bridge and cycled ahead to get the locks ready.

The first lock stood with its bottom gates open; Luke, on the lockside, beckoned him in. He let the *Swan* run gently between the gates, and looked back to see the *Tove* drifting towards him, Alice on the foredeck coiling in the towrope as it fell slack. As he stopped the motor, its stem against the top cill, Luke had the gates closed and hurried to open the top paddles. As he rose in the lock, he looked back to see the towline draped over the top of the bottom gates, still attached to the top of the butty's mast; then the top gates swung open, and Luke waved him forward:

'Stop it roight outsoide the lock! Don' troy 'n run on.' He nodded at the shouted command, and did as he was told; looking back again, all became clear to him: The one-hundred-foot-long towline now stretched from the stern of his motor boat, right over the entire length of the lock, and then dipped to tht top of the butty mast where it sat tucked into the vee of the bottom gates. Annie and Alice were quickly raising the bottom paddles, the lock draining again to allow the butty to enter; he slipped the clutch in, the engine running at tick-over, and drew the towline tight. And then, as the weight of water came off of the bottom gates, the butty gently nosed its way into the lock. He let the motor run slowly ahead, but then knocked the clutch out again, allowing it to drift to a stop; behind him, the butty rode up to the top gates, gently bumping against the cill.

Top paddles up again; the butty rose in the lock, and then they were away, moving on to the second lock where again Luke had the bottom gates standing open ready for him. The procedure was repeated, Jess almost chuckling to himself at the simple ingenuity of what they were doing; and then they were off on the three-mile run to the bottom lock of the flight at Audlem.

'That's what yeh calls long-linin' is it?' He asked Luke, now standing beside him on the gunwale. The older boy grinned at him:

'Yeah! S'easy, ain't it?'

'Yeah – it's obvious, once yeh've seen it done. So simple!'

'S'easy ter get it wrong though, mate. Go too 'ard wi' the motor 'n yeh can snap the line; not 'ard enough 'n it don' get inter the lock. Yeh did joost foine there, moind.'

Jess felt his spirits soar – much as he liked Luke, the other boy wasn't often free with his praise. Even now, he added a comment that deflated Jess somewhat:

'Not as quick as Abel would'a done it. But then it's better ter tek it slow 'n get it roight, Oi s'pose. They been doin' it fer a few years now.'

'Would you 'ave tried ter go any quicker? For yer first time?' Luke looked at him and chuckled; he shook his head:

'Nah! Oi'd be playin' it safe 'n all.'

And Jess was to get a lot more practice that day. Fifteen locks at Audlem; then five more at Adderley. It was as they approached the town of Market Drayton, with dusk rapidly closing in, that Luke peered ahead and let out a groan:

'Oh, 'Ell!' Jess looked at his friend, riding again on the gunwale at his side:

'What's up?'

'See them boats?' Luke gestured in front of them: 'That's ruddy 'Ampson's pair! They didn't go ter Middlewich after all.'

Jess could make out little of the boats at such a distance – but the plume of smoke over the towpath hedge told its own tale.

'That begger'll 'old oos oop all the ruddy way, you see if 'e don't!'

And true to form, as they came up behind the dirty, battered boats they saw Joe, at the helm of the motor now, glance back and then studiously ignore them. Bert Hampson, standing at his side, looked back once or twice, obviously urging his son to drive on and not give way.

'I wonder 'ow far 'e's goin?' Jess speculated.

'Ruddy Birnigum, knowin' ar luck!'

Once more, as they came up behind the other pair, Jess was forced to ease down the throttle and chug along behind them. And again, Annie came to the front of the butty and called across the intervening distance to ask what was holding them up. Informed, she shrugged her ample shoulders:

'Ah well – it's gettin' late. We'll stop in Drayton – mebbe we'll get by 'em termorrer.'

Luke turned to Jess:

'Mebbe we will – there's long straight lengths once we're through Drayton Locks, mebbe we can push ar way by 'im even if 'e don' want ter let oos.'

'Is that allowed?' Luke shrugged:

'T'ain't what yeh'd call polite – but if 'e won' loose oos by, what else can we do? We can' afford ter sit be'ind 'im all day.'

Chapter Eighteen

That morning, Hampson's boats had started out about two hours ahead of them. The *Constance* and the *Prudence* had spent the night tied just below the staircase locks of Bunbury; once the tired engine was going, Joe had taken the boats through, the locks worked by his parents and the two youngest. Jimmie was still feeling sorry for himself, but for a different reason now: the ten-year-old had woken up with a runny nose and a sore throat; quickly diagnosed by his mother – 'yeh've got a bit of a chill' – and he'd sipped some weak tea before being told to stay in the cabin and keep warm. Now, dozing fitfully, he lay quiet and still, curled up on his parents' bed wrapped in a blanket, trying not to sneeze.

Once again, they had worked on for an hour and a half after seeing the Clayton boats tie up behind them, into the deepening darkness, finally stopping by Tyrley Wharf at the top of the five Drayton locks.

'Ow!'

'Get oop then 'n get outta the ruddy way if yeh don' wanna get stood on!'

Jimmie Hampson wriggled beneath the folded-down flap of the cross-bed in the *Constance* as his older brother stood up. Dragging his blanket in after him, he curled up into a ball and tried to get comfortable.

He'd had little sleep – at first, his nose bunged up with his cold, he'd tossed and turned beside Joe until the teenager had lost patience and kicked him out, telling him to sleep on the floor. There, with just the worn-out rag rug under him for comfort, he'd become too hot and sweaty in the warm, stuffy night, until he'd thrown off the blanket and wriggled out of his underclothes. Even then, he'd only managed to sleep fitfully, continually woken by his inability to breathe. Now, as the light of the early morning crept in through the porthole above Bertie where he slept on the sidebed, he felt even more awful than he had the day before.

Grey daylight streamed in suddenly as Joe let himself out of the cabin, leaving the doors and the slide-hatch open. Bertie, wide awake, swung his legs to the floor and reached for his own clothes:

''Ow yeh feelin', Jimmie?'

'Ruddy 'orrible' Jimmie groaned.

'Tell Mam, shall Oi?'

'Yeah, please, Bertie.'

The eight-year-old chuckled, amused like any kid at his older brother's discomfiture. He dressed hurriedly and disappeared after Joe. A couple of minutes later, their mother appeared in the open hatches with a mug of weak tea; she came inside and sat on the step:

'There y'are Jimmie.' The boy clambered out from under the cross-bed; he reached for the tea gratefully and sipped at it, sitting on the edge of the sidebed. His mother gazed at him:

'Yeh still feelin' rough?' He nodded. 'Yeh'd better coom wi' me agen terday then. Bring yer blanket 'n curl oop on ar bed in the butty where Oi can keep an eye on yeh.' He nodded again. Finishing his tea, he carefully clambered out of the cabin and across into the butty, still

112

clad only in his blanket, where Enid had quickly straightened their bed, laying a spare cover over it for him to settle on.

. By the time Jimmie emerged, his father was trying to start the reluctant engine; and by the time it was going, they had lost half an hour of their advantage.

***

The *Swan* and the *Tove* were away promptly in the early dawn again, quickly covering the mile from the town to Drayton Locks. Up the flight, Luke steering today, Jess ahead on the old bike, Alice and her mother working the locks as Rosie proudly steered the butty, and they were off into the long eighteen-mile pound to Wheaton Aston.

That long stretch of the Shropshire Union Canal was among the last canals to be built in Britain – it used the latest technology of the early nineteenth century, driving through the countryside on high embankments and deep cuttings unlike older canals that followed the contours of the land. It is quite spectacular – but the long straight channel can become boring when you travel it week in, week out. After a couple of hours, Luke turned to Jess with a grin:

''Ere – you tek over fer a bit. Fancy a cuppa if Oi go down 'n brew oop?'

'Yeah, please!' Jess cheerfully took the tiller as Luke ducked down into the cabin.

They were running through the long curving cutting at Grub Street; by the time Luke emerged with two mugs

113

of tea they were emerging again into open countryside. The heavy boats swept on, the Bolinder driving them forward at full power making easy going of the deep channel. But the drawback of that was that they were rapidly overhauling the boats in front of them...

Chapter Nineteen

Past the little village of Norbury; two miles on, the bigger town of Gnosall quickly followed by the short Cowley Tunnel. In the cutting that soon follows, as they passed beneath the strange double arch of High Onn Bridge, Luke spotted smoke in the distance:

'Oh, 'Ell! Look there – it's 'Ampsons agen, we've caught 'em oop!'

And a mile on, as the cutting fell away to level ground, they were slowing down again, chugging along in the wake of the slower boats. A long straight lay in front of them – under a couple more bridges, and then they could see a long way ahead. Luke turned to Jess; he hesitated, but then said:

'We can' go on loike this! Go on Jess, woind it oop, get past 'em.' Jess looked at his friend, doubtful if that was a good idea, but Luke urged him on: 'Go on! There's nothin' coomin' th'other way, 'n if we gets oop with 'im 'e'll 'ave ter give way.'

Jess, still feeling unsure, wound the throttle full on again and pulled the oil rod all the way out, giving the big Bolinder all the power it had. Beneath him, the *Swan* surged forward, rapidly overtaking the *Prudence,* and they saw Joe look back from the helm of the *Constance* as he heard their engine pick up speed. The teenager shrugged, and turned his boats a little closer to the towpath, and Luke chuckled:

''E's loosin' oos by! Oi told yeh 'e would once 'e saw oos coomin'.'

But then Bert Hampson looked back too, and turned to his son, cuffing him around the ear. What was obviously an argument ensued on the other motor boat, and after a moment they saw a cloud of grey smoke burst from its exhaust pipe as Joe opened the throttle as far as he could. Luke swore:

'Stoopid beggar! 'E's tryin' ter race oos!'

'Shall I 'old back?' Jess asked.

'No! Keep goin', damn him, we got enough ter get past any'ow.'

By now they were drawing alongside the *Prudence,* Enid Hampson looking back at them, her face expressionless. The *Swan* continued to overhaul her; they were right beside the dirty, battered butty when it gave sudden lurch towards them, rolling partly onto its side, and abruptly stopped. The towline to the *Constance* parted with an audible twang, and part of it came flying back to whip around the butty's mast; startled, Jess slammed the oil rod in and wound off his throttle, allowing the *Swan* to lose speed quickly. He glanced back; Annie had seen what was happening and had swung the *Tove* over to the far bank, letting its bow rub along in the undergrowth to slow it down and keep the towline tight.

Beside them, the *Prudence* was still leaning over at a frightening angle, its near gunwale not far above the water; at the stern, Enid was hanging on, her face a fearful mask. Jess snatched out the clutch and hurriedly reversed his engine, ready to set back and help the obviously distressed boatwoman.

'What on earth...' Jess turned to Luke as the *Swan* came to a halt.

'She's 'it somethin' under the water' Luke said: 'Run oop on it 'n stuck there. Back oop 'n we'll get Missus 'Ampson off.'

Jess was letting the boat trickle slowly backwards; looking behind them, he saw Alice on the front of the *Tove,* ready to coil in their towline – Annie had obviously guessed their next move. He brought the *Swan* carefully backwards, allowing it to run close alongside the stricken butty; Luke made his way around the gunwale onto the flat deck in front of the cabin, gesturing for him to put him close to where Enid still stood, shocked and scared, in the well behind the cabin. He brought the boat to a halt again, right next to the *Prudence;* looking around, he thought that the butty seemed to be leaning over even more now. He puzzled about this for a moment before realisation struck and horrified him: *It's sinkin'! Must 'ave knocked a 'ole in the bottom...*

Luke leant over to Enid and grabbed her by both arms; she scrambled across onto the *Swan's* deck, where she sat down abruptly and put her face in her hands. He had rescued her just in time; at that moment, the *Prudence* rolled over towards them, pushing the *Swan* away, and sank on its side, leaving just the one side of the hull and cabin barely above water. Looking around, Luke saw the *Constance,* still some distance away in front of them, Joe at the helm reversing the boat towards them. He knelt down beside Enid:

117

'Missus 'Ampson? Are you all roight?' She looked up at him, her eyes still frightened, but she nodded jerkily:

'Yeah, Oi'm h'okay.' She turned as Jess came to join them and smiled up at them: 'Thank yeh fer stoppin' 'n 'elpin'...'

'Weren't goin' ter leave yeh, were we?' Luke told her.

'Where's moy man?' She gazed around and spotted the *Constance,* slowly running back but still some way away, Joe and Bert at the stern, and two small faces peering back over the cabin. Suddenly, a look of horror came into her eyes:

'Jimmie! JIMMIE!' She turned to the sunken butty: *'JIMMIE!'*

'What is it, Missus 'Ampson?' Luke asked urgently, already guessing the terrible truth.

''E's in there! In the cabin – 'e weren't feelin' well, 'n 'e was lyin' down on ar bed...'

***

Feeling pretty awful, and very sorry for himself, Jimmie Hampson had settled down in the butty cabin as his parents and siblings had got the boats under way. He'd nibbled at a slice of bread, relieving the pangs in his tummy a bit, and then curled up on his mother's bed, wrapping himself in the blanket. He'd been rather too warm during the night, but now, with the cabin doors and slide open, the chill of the morning made him shiver a little; and his clothes were all in the other cabin. But

118

snuggling down, he soon began to feel comfortable again, and after his sleepless night, he was soon drifting off, lulled by the easy motion of the boat and the gentle sound of the water rippling along its hull.   The hours passed as he dozed, the distant sound of the *Constance's* engine only making him feel even more sleepy...

Suddenly the boat gave a violent lurch under him. Barely half-awake, he puzzled for a moment at where he was, and what had happened to stir him. Something felt wrong, but he was still so sleepy; and he could still hear the gurgling of the water, so everything must be all right...   Slipping away into slumber again, still that feeling of something being wrong nagged at him, and he rolled over onto his back, stretched his legs out under the blanket – and jerked upright: His feet were above his head! Why...?

And then he was falling backwards, his head hitting the wall behind him, bundling into a ball as gravity forced him into the corner; and suddenly cold – and wet. The water flooding the cabin brought him to his senses as instinct made him hold his breath. Unsure which way was up, tangled in his blanket, he struggled to get free, to find some air; he fought the seemingly malicious cloth as it swirled around him, defeating his every attempt to kick it away.   He felt himself getting weaker, and struggled harder to get free – he had to breathe – but he couldn't – he was trapped...   His struggles became weaker, and then a warm darkness overcame him, and he let himself slip down into its embrace...

Chapter Twenty

Jess and Luke stared at the woman in horror.

''E's still in there?' Luke asked; she just nodded, distraught. The cabin was virtually under water, just one side showing; for a moment, they all stood rigid with shock. Then Jess quickly threw off his coat and kicked off his boots; he dived into the water that separated the two boats, swam around to the stern of the upturned *Prudence,* and dived to get through the open cabin doors.

Inside, it was suddenly dark, and he felt his way in. Something was blocking his way forward, something long and round; he felt about it, and realised that it was the chimney of the stove – the range itself had broken free of its mountings and fallen across the cabin, dragging the flue with it so that it now lay across his path at an angle. He heaved at it, then turned and kicked hard – it broke free and fell out of the way, and he pushed past it into the farther part of the cabin, to the crossbed where the boy had been lying. Groping around, at first he couldn't find Jimmie, and began to wonder if Enid had been mistaken in her distress and shock.

But then his foot touched something warm and soft, and he kicked himself around to feel beneath him. And now he had the boy, curled up in a ball in the corner of the bed, unmoving... A pocket of air had been trapped under the high side of the cabin wall, and now he thrust his head up into it and drew a deep breath before plunging down under the water again. Working as quickly as he could, he dragged the obstructing blanket away from the boy's nude body and wrapped his arms

120

around him. He used his feet to push himself up, and fought his way back to the doors where he thrust the unconscious youngster through before him.

Eager hands grabbed Jimmie away from him, and he emerged himself, gasping for breath, and climbed over onto the deck of the *Swan*. Luke had laid the boy on his back and bent over him; he looked up at Jess, his expression anguished:

''E ain't breathin', Jess!' Jess knelt beside him; he felt at Jimmie's throat, and found a weak pulse.

''E's still alive, just abaht! 'Elp me, Luke.' They rolled the boy onto his face, and Jess threw his weight against his back, trying to force the water from his lungs. He got no response, and paused, looking hopelessly around at Luke; but then he tried again, once, twice, three times, putting his full weight on the boy's chest. And suddenly Jimmie gave a cough, and water gushed from his mouth. He coughed again, gasped, and coughed up more water; he drew a deep, shuddering breath, and Jess looked up to meet Luke's eyes:

'Get my blanket outta the cabin, Luke.' He knew that the wet, naked boy would quickly become dangerously chilled; Luke hurried to fetch it as he helped Jimmie to turn over again and sit up, leaning forward with his head on his raised knees.

Enid had leapt to her feet as her son had been dragged onto the deck, and stood distraught as Jess had tried to revive him; now she too knelt beside her son and grabbed him into her arms, murmuring his name:

'Jimmie – Jimmie, oh Jimmie...' She looked around at Jess, gazed into his dark eyes for a moment: 'Thank yeh, boy, thank yeh! Yeh saved moy kiddie..'

Jess shrugged his shoulders, embarrassed at her gratitude, as Luke returned with the blanket. She took it from him and lovingly wrapped her son in it before putting her arms around him and hugging him tightly, rocking gently back and forth:

'Jimmie, Jimmie – yeh're all roight, yeh're safe now – oh, Jimmie...'

A bump heralded the arrival of the *Constance* alongside the *Swan,* and they all looked up. Bert Hampson, his face dark with fury, stepped across onto the deck and drew himself up in front of Luke:

'Whad'ya think yeh're doin' boy? Yeh push oos outta yer way, troyin' ter barge past, 'n run moy butty on summat – now look, yeh've soonk it! Yeh'll pay fer this, Luke Kain, 'n you, Mister ruddy Carter!'

Neither of them replied, too astonished at his attitude to gather their thoughts. But Enid got slowly to her feet and turned to face her husband, her fists clenched at her side:

'YOU SHUT OOP, BERT 'AMPSON! THAT LAD'S JOOST SAVED YER SON'S LOIFE – IF'N YEH CAN'T BE GRATEFUL, AT LEAST KEEP YER RUDDY TRAP SHUT! 'N DON' YOU DARE GO BLAMIN' THEM FER WHAT'S 'APPENED – IF YEH WEREN'T SO RUDDY H'IGNORANT 'N PIG-'EADED THIS WOULD NEVER 'AVE 'APPENED!'

They all stared at her, astonished at her outburst, her husband not least of all. His mouth hung open in surprise; he shut it and drew breath:

'Enid...'

'Don' you Enid me!' She bridled at him: 'This is it, Bert 'Ampson, Oi've 'ad enough, do yeh hear! If yeh'd done the sensible thing 'n loosed these fellas by when yeh saw they were quicker'n oos, we wouldn' be in this mess! It's yer own fault ar boy nearly drownded – it's yer fault too that ar 'ome's on its soide under the ruddy water! Well now yeh can tek care o' yerself! Oi've 'ad enough!' she repeated. She paused for breath – no-one spoke into the tense silence until she went on again, now in slightly calmer tones:

'It's thanks ter you drinkin' all the money we gets that yeh've got ar Joe stealin' to put food on the table! 'N yeh h'ain't got the money ter fix the h'injun nor look after the boats what we depends on fer ar livin'! It's no good, Bert, it can' go on, Oi tells yeh.'

'But...' Hampson was lost for words, and by now both Luke and Jess were recovering from the shock of Enid's tirade and trying not to laugh at the bully's discomfiture and his shocked expression. But Enid wasn't finished:

'Oi means it, Bert 'Ampson! Yeh're on yer own now, Oi'm tekin' the kiddies 'n we're goin' ter mek ar own way. It ain't far ter Wheaton, we'll walk it from 'ere, 'n we'll get a bus back ter the Port 'n stay wi' moy sister 'n 'ers 'til we gets sorted. If you 'n Joe wants ter tek the motor 'n h'unload what yeh got left o' the load that's oop ter you.'

123

She stopped talking, and no-one quite dared to say anything. She looked around, as if surprised at her own outburst, and caught sight of Annie standing on the towpath opposite the stricken butty.

'If there's anythin' we can do ter 'elp, Enid...'

'Oi know, Annie. Thank yeh.' The two women exchanged smiles, and Enid bent to her son again, taking him in her arms. She looked up at her eldest: 'Joe – go 'n get some clothes fer Jimmie, will yeh, 'fore 'e catches 'is death.'

Chapter Twenty-One

'Yeh've got a bit of a problem, 'ave yeh?'

Everyone turned around again at the sound of a raised voice. Amongst all the hullabaloo, none of them had heard the sound of the approaching engine, or noticed the boat ease to a halt close in front of the two stopped motors. A single motor boat, in the red and green colours of Fellows, Morton & Clayton Ltd, the name *Otter* emblazoned on its fore-cabin, sat with its fore-end between those of the *Swan* and the *Constance*, its steerer now standing on its foredeck looking at the figures gathered on the deck of the oil-boat.

'Aye! Butty's 'it summat on the bottom 'n gone down.' Luke was the one to reply – Hampson was still too shocked at his wife's sudden vehemence.

'Roight. What can we do ter 'elp?' Luke looked around:

'Not a lot, mate. We've got a load o' h'oil fer Langley so we needs ter be gettin' ahead.'

'Ah. 'Oo's boats are they?' Hampson finally stirred himself:

'Them's moine.'

'What yeh got on?'

'H'iron ore, fer Wolver'ampton.'

'Oh boy! Go rusty down there, it will!' The man chuckled, but Hampson's expression said that he didn't appreciate the humour. He went on: 'H'okay – you stay 'ere wi the boats, 'n we'll stop at Gnosall 'n tellyphone the coomp'ny, mek sure as they knows 'bout yer troubles. Shift yer motor out o' the way, onto the towpath, mate.'

Grudgingly, Hampson made to do as he suggested, but Joe dived down into the cabin. He re-emerged moments later, a bundle of clothes under his arm. He held something out to Jess:

''Ere, Jess.' Jess took it, surprised – and then realised he was holding his own best shirt. He looked up meet the other boy's ashamed gaze:

'What...?' Joe held up his hand:

'Yeh saved moy kid brother from that cabin. It's little enough, ter give yeh back what's your'n anyway, but it's all Oi got. Thank yeh fer savin' ar Jimmie.' He gave the other things to his mother and turned away quickly to run the length of the top-planks, jumping down onto the foredeck of his boat ready to moor it against the towpath as his father pushed the lever into forward gear. Jess watched as they moved the boat clear, around the waiting FMC motor, and tied it up with pins hammered into the bank. The Fellows's boatman went to go past, but Enid called out to him:

'Can yeh give oos a lift, mate?'

'Where to?'

'Where yeh goin'?'

'Audlem, ternoight. Ter the Port termorrer, wi' luck.'

'Can yeh drop oos ter Audlem, then? Me 'n the kiddies?'

'Yeah, Oi s'pose so – but...'

''E can look after 'imself!' She gestured at Hampson, and then called out to her oldest son: 'Will you stay wi' yer dad, Joe, ter 'elp 'im? Yeh can coom 'n join the rest of oos later, if yeh wants.'

'Will yeh be h'okay, Enid?' Annie asked; the other boatwoman laughed:

'We'll mek out, you see! We'll get the bus ter the Port from Audlem, 'n Beryl'll tek os in fer now. Oi'll get the boys' things from the motor when Bert gets it back there – moine 'n Maggie's'll be ruined any'ow.'

''Ave ye got any money ter toide yeh over?'

'Ah! Oh...' That made Enid stop suddenly. She gave a rueful smile: 'Oi did 'ave! It's in there' she pointed to the upturned butty cabin.

Jess was still wet through, holding his best shirt in his hand; he gave her a pained look:

'Where is it, Missus 'Ampson?'

'It were in a purse, one 'e...' she gestured at Bert again: 'Didn' know about, tucked in a biscuit tin in the table-cupboard.'

''Old this.' He gave his shirt to Luke, and turned and dived into the water again. Ducking back inside the drowned cabin, he felt his way past the space where the range had once stood to the upright structure, now part of the ceiling above him, of the table-cupboard. Unclipping the fold-down door, he drew back as a cascade of tins, plates, cups and other implements rained down out of it. He put his head above water, into the trapped air-pocket again, and took a deep breath. Then under once more; looking around, he spotted a battered old biscuit tin lying among the piled crockery. Quickly wrenching it open, he grabbed the worn leather purse from within.

127

Enid knelt down to help him back up onto the deck of the *Swan* as he reappeared from her cabin. He handed her the purse, and she threw her arms around him, not caring how wet he was:

'Bless you, boy! Yeh saved moy Jimmie, 'n now yeh've found me savin's too! Thank yeh, Jess!' He shrugged, smiling a little shyly at her:

'I'm 'appy ter 'elp, 'n that Jimmie's all right. Good thing I learnt ter swim!' She held him at arm's length, her own smile radiant:

'It is that, boy. Wherever we ends oop, me 'n the kiddies, yeh'll alwes foind a welcome wi' oos. Bless you, Jess Carter.' She drew him close and kissed him on the cheek.

Luke stood looking on, a broad smile on his face:

'Missus 'Ampson? Tek Jimmie down in ar cabin 'n get 'im dressed 'fore 'e catches 'is death. Then if yeh're h'okay, we'll 'ave ter get goin'.'

'Thank yeh, Luke.' She hustled the boy down inside, calling out to her younger children: 'Bertie! Maggie! Get yerselves off that boat'n back 'ere wi' me!'

They did as they were told, jumping onto the towpath and hurrying back to where their submerged butty lay. The boatman on the *Otter* drew his boat clear and over against the bank to allow them to scramble aboard, and then moved back alongside the *Swan*. When Enid and Jimmie emerged again, the boy now dressed in his working clothes, he went shyly up to Jess:

'Mam says yeh saved my loife?' Jess shrugged his shoulders, but he smiled at the youngster who stood

128

gazing admiringly up into his eyes, shivering still from the shock of his ordeal:

'I guess so, Jimmie.'

'Thank yeh...' Wide eyes looked up at him, and then the boy threw his arms around him: 'Thank yeh!' Jess extricated himself, embarrassed all over again:

'It's okay Jimmie. I couldn' leave yeh in there, could I?' Jimmie shook his head:

'Oi'll never ferget what yeh did fer me, Jess!' Jess gently pushed him away:

'Go on wi' yer Mam now. Be good, eh?'

Her children gathered on the *Otter,* Enid too stepped across the gunwales with a last wave to Jess and Luke. As the FMC motor drew past on its way northwards, the boatman ushered her and Jimmie down into his cabin to let the boy get warm and recover from his shock. Before she disappeared inside, she called across:

'You coom 'n see oos when yeh're back at the Port, yeh hear, boys?'

Chapter Twenty-Two

Half an hour later, the *Swan* and the *Tove* were on their way once more, leaving just Bert Hampson and his oldest son to watch over their boats until the canal company's crew arrived to rescue them.

Luke had taken over the *Swan's* tiller again, backed up and picked up the tow, setting off for the two miles to Wheaton Aston village and its single lock; Jess spent the next half-hour in the cabin, stripping off his wet clothes, towelling himself down and dressing again in his spare shirt and trousers. He was out again in time to jump off at Tavern Bridge and pedal quickly on to set the lock, an easy task as other oncoming boats had left it in their favour.

The lock passed, watercans filled, they ate a delayed meal on the long pound past the town of Brewood and on to the junction and stop-lock at Autherley. Alice took the opportunity, delivering their loaded plates, to swap boats and ride on the motor in order to talk to Jess about what had happened. Rosie tried to join her, but Annie put her foot down:

'You stay 'ere wi' me, Rosie, yeh can talk ter Jess later.'

On the *Swan,* Alice sat beside Jess on the deck in front of the cabin while he ate his dinner; Luke stood at the tiller, his own plate on the slide hatch in front of him, tucking in with gusto as he steered the boat along the straight pound. Once Jess had eaten, she plied him with questions – from her perch in the hatches of the butty, she'd followed much of what had happened, but he still had to go over it in detail to satisfy her curiosity. She burst out laughing when he told her about Enid's furious tirade at her husband:

'From what Oi 'ear, 'e 'ad it coomin' to 'im! Little Maggie said as they never 'ave enough ter eat 'cause 'er dad's alwes drunk the money – serves 'im roight! Oi 'ope they'll be h'okay, though.'

'Yeah, me too. I kinda like little Jimmie – 'n even Joe seemed like 'e might be okay, underneath. 'Is dad's the rough'un, I reckon.'

The story told, they lapsed into a companionable silence, sitting quietly enjoying the afternoon sunshine.

It was getting late in the day by the time they had turned onto the Staffs and Worcester Canal at Autherley; half a mile on, and they turned again, left now, under the old brick bridge and into the first lock of the long flight that led up to the centre of Wolverhampton. Rosie dashed off to the stables, but came back disappointed:

'They ain't got no spare 'orses, Mam!'

'Never moind Rosie, we'll long-line 'em' Luke consoled her, aware that she had been looking forward to working with a horse again – a number were kept at the bottom of the Wolverhampton locks for use by the boaters, to pull their butties up the twenty-one, making their long uphill haul easier and faster. But this time they were out of luck.

Into the flight, through the first quite rural locks; then they approached the immense arch of the perhaps-inappropriately named Spring Bridge, carrying the railway high above their heads. Below it, into the next lock, and now their luck changed – a horse appeared from under Gorsebrook bridge, a small boy astride its broad back.

He drew to a halt beside them:

''Allo! D'yer want the 'orse?' He hailed Luke, on the motor.

'Yeah! From the stables at the bottom, is 'e?'

'S'roight. This is Jutland – 'e's a good 'orse! 'E'll get yer butty ter the top in no toime, 'n yeh doesn' 'ave ter tek 'im back – 'e'll foind 'is own way if yeh joost sets 'im off.' Alice had come over, and stroked the animal's nose:

'Is that roight?' The stocky brown pony flicked his ears as if in confirmation.

'Yeah! Oi loikes ter 'ave a break from ar boats,'n moy Pa let's me tek 'im back. Oi've got sixpence fer the bus, ter catch oop wi' them. If you 'as 'im from 'ere, Oi can 'ave meself a coupl'a pennies!' Luke reached up for the boy's hand:

'All roight, we'll 'ave 'im, thanks! Yeh're sure as 'e'll mek 'is own way back without oos 'avin' ter tek 'im?' The kid slid down to the ground:

'Yeah! Joost let 'im go, tell 'im ter go 'ome.'

'H'okay, thanks – what's yer name?'

'Johnnie – Johnnie Barnet. We're wi' Fellers's, got the *Lily* 'n the *Norway,* wi' spelter fer the foundry by Fact'ry Turn. Yeh won' tell moy Pa Oi was ridin' 'im, will yeh?' Luke laughed:

'We'll keep yer secret, Johnnie!'

'Thanks! Yeh coom from the Port, 'ave yeh?'

'Yeah, s'roight – we got h'oil fer Langley.'

132

'Ah, Oi thought so! Oi saw yer boats there.' The boy glanced around at Jess, waiting by the open lock-gates: 'Oi've 'eard about you, ain't Oi? Yeh're the feller as jumped in the Ship Canal ter save that little girl!' Jess smiled resignedly, but Alice laughed:

''E's done it agen, 'n all! Rescued a kiddie from a sunken cabin, terday!' Johnnie's eyes grew wide:

'Did yeh really?' Jess nodded reluctantly, but he said:

'We'd better be gettin' on, 'adn't we, Luke?'

'Yeah, yeh're roight. Rosie – coom 'n look after Jutland 'ere, get 'im 'ooked oop ter the towline. Thanks, Johnnie – see yeh 'round, eh?'

'Yeah, sure!' The youngster dashed off with a last wave and an admiring look at Jess who just smiled at him as he ran past, and disappeared up onto the road bridge to find his bus.

The rest of the journey went more quickly and more easily now, with the placid, willing pony hauling the *Tove* up the flight. At the top, with the early summer twilight descending into darkness around them, they tied for the night; Rosie slipped an apple into Jutland's mouth and made a fuss of him before turning him around and telling him:

'Go on 'ome, Jutland! Go on now.' The horse turned to look at her as if saying 'I know what to do', tossed his head and set off at a gentle trot back the way they had come.

'This was where we got the fish 'n chips las' toime, remember?' Luke asked Jess, knowing that his mother would overhear – but she was having none of it:

'Ain't no good you droppin' 'ints, Luke Kain! Yeh've 'ad a good meal terday, 'n yeh've got cold sausages 'n bread fer supper. Oi'll get the kettle on fer tea.'

Chapter Twenty-Three

The next day saw their journey concluded. A couple of hours to Oldbury, and they swept past Clayton's yard to the junction with the Titford Canal – up the six locks of 'the Crow', around to the Shell depot at Langley Green, and then breakfast as the pumps slurped the oil out of their holds into the wharfside tanks. Down the locks again, around the corner, and they tied on the yard before lunchtime.

Annie quickly set up the dolly-tub again, chivvying her children, Jess included, out of their working clothes so that she could wash them.

'We goin' ter get off agen later, Mam?' Luke asked as he handed her his pile pf dirty clothes.

'No – we'll get goin' in the mornin'. That way we'll get ter the Port Sunday, joost in toime fer the tug on Monday, roight?'

'It's Thurday terday?' Jess queried; she nodded:

'Ah. We're a bit be'ind, after the 'old-oop yesterday, but if we can go termorrer, three days there, three days back, get a trip in every week, we won' be sittin' around waitin' fer the tug, roight?'

'Yeah – meks sense' Luke agreed.

'I'll 'ave time ter go 'n see my Dad, terday?' Jess asked; Annie chuckled:

'O'course, boy! We'll go on the bus, you 'n me, eh?'

'Yeah! Thanks, Mam.'

* * *

Ted Carter braced himself, gathering his son into his arms as the boy ran across the visiting room. The prison officers standing guard carefully turned a blind eye as they embraced – there were times when the 'no contact' rule could be quietly ignored. Annie Kain settled herself into one of the chairs by the small table and waited while father and son parted, Ted taking the seat facing them as Jess sat at her side.

'So Jesse – have yeh had a good trip?'

'Yes, thanks Dad. It went well, with our new boat. It broke down agen, on the way, but I fixed it meself!'

'You did? Clever kid!'

'Yeah – 'n the man at the Port said as I'd done a really good job too, when 'e checked it over fer us.'

'Good fer you, son! Makin' a name fer yerself, are yeh?' Annie chuckled at this:

'In more ways than one, 'n all!'

'Oh? What d'yeh mean, Annie?'

'Made a 'ero of 'imself agen, ain't 'e?' Ted raised his eyebrows; Jess was squirming with embarrassment:

'Oh Mam! It weren't nothin' really.' Ted gave him a quizzical look:

'Mam?' Annie reached across the table, took Ted's hand in her own:

'Oi 'ope yeh don' moind, Ted? It's h'easier if 'e calls me that, that's all, it don' mean nothin'.' Ted smiled at her:

'Pity! 'E could do with a mother ter look arter 'im. O'course I don't mind! Rowena's long gone now, 'n I guess you're the best person I could wish for to keep an eye on 'im for me.' He turned to Jess again: 'So what happened this time, Jesse?' Jess shrugged;

'It's a long story, Dad...'

'I've got all the time in the world, son!'

'Well, it started up at the Port...'

Half an hour later Ted sat back, looking admiringly over the table at his son:

'One thing I promise you, Jesse – when I get out of 'ere, I'm goin' ter keep my nose clean. No more drivin' fer gangsters; I'll get a proper job...' He hesitated: 'Mebbe I could even get a job around the canal, somewhere – that'd suit you, eh? I've been talkin ter people, askin' about things – 'n it's obvious 'ow much you like the life...' Jess was staring at him, a delighted grin on his face:

'That's what I've been thinkin' too, Dad! It'd be great, wouldn' it?' Ted held his hands up:

'Slow down! I'm goin' ter be in 'ere fer a while yet, don' ferget.' He turned to the boatwoman:

'Ann – you're happy to keep my boy on, part of your crew?'

'O'course Oi am, Ted...' She was struck, somewhat touched, by his use of her 'proper' name – everyone always called her 'Annie': ''E's one of oos now, whether 'e loikes it or not!'

'Thank you – and – you will keep coming to see me? Yerself, I mean?' She smiled at him:

'Jess 'as ter 'ave a grown-oop come with 'im, any'ow, they won' let 'im in, else.'

'That wasn't what I meant, Ann...' Her smile grew broader:

'Oi didn' think it was, Ted!' He stood up, and she too got to her feet: 'We better get goin', Jess.'

'Okay, Mam.' He stood up too, watching as his father took the boatwoman's hand, and then drew her close to kiss her on the cheek:

'I'll see you soon?'

'Yeh will, Ted. We'll be back next week, agen.'

Ted Carter embraced his son:

'Take care of yerself, Jess.'

'You too, Dad!' Carter laughed:

'Nothin' much can 'appen to me 'ere, can it!'

A BIT MORE EXPLANATION!

Once again, dear reader, there may be a few things in my story that I ought to explain. I'm going to assume you've read my other Jess Carter stories, so you know a lot already...?

You might be puzzled by the way I sometimes use different names for places, especially the locks. I tend to use the old boater's names in my tales, but today we often use different names – What the boatmen knew as 'Drayton Five' are better known now as 'Tyrley Locks'. And the boaters would have spoken of ''Ampton twenty-one', rather than Wolverhampton Locks. And I guess you've worked out that 'The Port' refers to Ellesmere Port – easy one, right?

Talking of locks – the 'Iron Lock' at Beeston is quite real, as some of you might have discovered if you've been that way. What I have said in the story is true – it replaced the previous stone-built locks because they kept falling in, and even the iron lock has moved over the years, so that the walls lean inwards from bottom to top. Which is why Abel Beechey told the boys that if they could get in with the boats empty, they'd be okay when they were loaded – loaded boats sit a lot lower in the water.

The geography of Ellesmere Port has changed a bit since the war, too. The level crossing's not there any more, the road goes up and over the railway on a long bridge now, and there's a nice new motorway that runs right by the old basins and warehouses of the canal, so a lot of the old streets that I've mentioned when Luke, Jess and Alice were exploring are gone. Porter's Row is still there, inside what is now the Museum complex. And the Wolverhampton Corrugated Iron Works? Yes, it used to be right there, alongside the railway lines! The company had moved there from Wolverhampton, hence the confusing name!

And Jutland? Yes, the canal company did keep a few horses stabled at the bottom of Wolverhampton Locks in those times. With 21 locks to be worked, bow-hauling or even long-lining a loaded butty uphill would have been a slow and arduous job – much quicker and easier if the motor could go on ahead, with a horse to tow the butty up behind. And some of those horses were so used to the job that they would indeed make their own way home from the top, once sent off that way.

Again, a few 'real' people appear in my story: Abel Beechey was one of Thomas Clayton's boatmen – he was in my first Jess Carter story, you'll remember? And Steve Dulson really did work his pair of horse-boats, until well after the war, with his grandchildren as crew. The other characters are all fictitious – the Hampsons, the people at Ellesmere Port, even Mike Parker. I don't know if there was a self-employed engineer at the Port, but there might well have been – and he helped me tell the story about Bert Hampson!

I hope you have enjoyed my tale – will there be another? Maybe...

Geoffrey Lewis

If you have enjoyed this story,
You might like to know that there are more Jess Carter books available! The first, Jess Carter & the Oil Boat, was published in 2010, and Jess Carter & the Bolinder in 2011.

And there are other Canal Novels from Geoffrey Lewis:
The Michael Baker Series
The four (so far) books of the popular Michael Baker Trilogy are also available, telling the story of a runaway who finds a new life and relearns trust and affection among the boating people during and after the Second World War
Starlight
is a tale of childhood friendship and loyalty, set in 1955 by the Oxford Canal – a lock-keeper's son who befriends a new arrival in the village and introduces him to the world of the waterways.
'A beautiful tale, beautifully told'

Also coming later in 2013:
'Remember Me'
A collection of deeply moving short stories centred on a novella set in the Australian Outback, on a theme of personal loss and renewal.

www.sgmpublishing.co.uk